I0623253

Foreword

Mitch Taylor and Rebecca Sorenson share a secret.

Rebecca's job is rewarding as secretary of Cascade Elementary—the same school she attended as a child. She has a great group of friends, even though many of whom are married now. And if sometimes she wished she was up there in that sparkling white dress...

Except, wait—she did get to wear bridal white. Granted, it was a slinky party dress and the justice of the peace was Elvis in a gold lame jacket, but still, the deed was done.

She'd tied the knot.

Mitch Taylor doesn't do regrets. It would be a waste of energy bemoaning the mistakes he'd made in his life. The end of his promising football career taught him nothing in life was a guarantee.

Like love.

What were the chances two people from the same po-dunk town in Washington would end up together in a nightclub in Las Vegas? A few too many drinks later, a hasty ceremony performed by the king of rock 'n' roll, and they'd been hitched. The night that followed lived on in his dreams, but when he'd woken the next morning she was gone.

Can these two mismatched lovers find a way past their mistakes, or will they keep their lonely hearts guarded forever?

I have so many people I'd like to thank. First and foremost my husband, Robert John. Without you I wouldn't have had the courage to pursue my dreams. Thank you.

My mom, who has always been my guiding light and allows me to toss ideas with her. Thank you.

To my daughter, Brandy; you are my inspiration to never give up.

To my critique buddies, you know who you are. Without you pushing me to better myself, this book might never have happened.

To my beta readers for their tremendous input, and the reviewers who are key to a writer's success, thank you.

And last but not least, to Kim Killion and Jennifer Jakes, for the beautiful cover I'm so proud of and the services you provide. Thank you.

This book marks the fifth in the Wounded Hearts series centered around the citizens of Tidal Falls, Washington. The characters have grown and taken on a life of their own and I've had great fun getting to know them.

I hope you enjoy Mitch and Rebecca's story.

Jacquie

Introduction

Rebecca was in Hell.

What other explanation could there be for the reappearance of Mitch in her life when she'd worked so diligently to avoid him for the best part of eighteen hundred and eighteen days—not that she was counting.

The divorce papers sitting on the desk at home were burning a hole through her brain, making her ache with things she dared not admit.

He looked amazing, by far the handsomest man in a room full of fine-looking men. His white dress shirt emphasized the breadth of those impossibly wide shoulders, honed to steel by years of honest manual labor. But then she'd always admired that about him. When his football career had come to an abrupt end he could have turned to a bottle and no one would have faulted him for it. Instead he picked himself up, went to a community college, got his welding ticket, and opened a business. Now his work was often sought after from all over the state and his shop had grown from a backyard garage to a fully equipped warehouse on a prime piece of Tidal Falls land. Mitch Taylor was a local success story.

He grasped her hand and she reluctantly followed his lead across a floor now packed with swaying bodies. He didn't stop until they reached a shadowed alcove off to one side of the stage. When he turned and held out his arms she stepped forward like a lamb, letting his jacket drop onto a nearby chair. The moment his arms wrapped around her and his calloused fingers found the bare skin of her lower back, Becky knew she was in trouble.

Her startled gaze rushed upward and tangled in the molten heat of his amber eyes. The light and shadows created by their surroundings turned his face lean and mysterious and oh-so-hypnotic. Someone bumped into them but she barely noticed, she was so caught up in his aura. It had been like this before—in Las Vegas.

Rebecca tried to pull away, her heart beating double time, an out-of-sync counterpoint to the drums playing on stage. Mitch simply tugged so that she had to grasp the front of his shirt to keep from falling— not that he would have let her. There were many things about Mitch Taylor that bothered her, but she never doubted his kindness.

He bowed his head and rested his cheek against her temple and his voice rumbled through her soul. "It's just a dance, sweetheart. What are you afraid of?"

Everything.

Him.

Herself.

Chapter 1

Would this day never end? Rebecca Sorenson shuffled the papers on her desk and glanced up at the school clock for the tenth time in so many minutes. She had plans, big plans and couldn't wait to get a start on the weekend.

Tonight was the big night for her best friend, Annie's, bachelorette celebration. Which is why—Rebecca glanced at the clock again just as the bell rang signaling classes were done—she needed to get going. There was still a ton of last minute preparations before the party.

She hurried to log off the computer, finished stacking her secretarial files, and reached into the bottom drawer for her hobo styled handbag and striped sun hat. Annie made fun of the fact she had to give up two pay-checks to afford her purse with its straw look and leather straps, but hello, *Jimmy Choo*. She wouldn't call herself vain exactly, but she definitely preferred good quality whenever she could afford it.

The elementary kids poured out of their classrooms, laughing and talking, not a worry on their sweet minds. Rebecca envied them their youth. Life had a way of bleeding that exuberance away.

Okay, enough with the maudlin shit.

She pasted a smile on her lips and rounded the end of the counter to join the melee heading for the front entrance.

"Bye, Miss Sorenson," little Jessica Reed sang as she rushed past with a couple of friends in tow.

Becky's heart pinched. She loved each and every one of the precious little rug-rats. Outside parents stood in friendly groups chatting, some with strollers or fussy preschoolers tugging on their hands. The moment they caught sight of their children, welcoming smiles broke out and arms opened wide to hug them close. The gentlest of breezes, just enough to take the heat out of the early summer sunshine, teased the girls' dresses and flirted with the boys' jackets. It was like a Hallmark movie.

She lifted the strap of her purse higher, plunked her hat on her head, and dodged families as she made her way across the playground, intent on reaching the bike rack where her prized baby blue Schwinn waited with a sturdy padlock.

A boy, maybe grade three going by his size, was crouched near the back tire of a beat-up black bike covered in superhero decals. He looked near tears as he fought to free the bike from its lock. Rebecca hesitated, anxious to get going, but the kid's obvious turmoil tugged at her heart.

"Hi," she said brightly. "Looks like you have a problem there. Can I help?"

The boy looked up at her through the thickest set of dark lashes and puppy dog eyes. She moved closer and his grubby fingers covered the combination while his gaze became even more fearful.

Rebecca stopped and raised her hands. "It's okay, kiddo, I work here." She pointed at the school behind them. "In the office. I'm Miss Sorenson. What's your name?"

He looked down, wiped his nose with the sleeve of his jacket, and mumbled, "Tommy."

Becky crouched and set her purse beside her on the tarmac. She knew most of the children attending Cascade Elementary, but not this little guy.

"What class are you in, Tommy?"

He flushed and looked toward the kids romping on the playground. When he turned back his face was belligerent. "I don't go to this dumb school."

Well, that explained why she didn't recognize him. She started to rise, saw the hint of desperation in his gaze, and stilled.

She nodded toward the bicycle. "That's a pretty terrific bike you have there. Do you want me to try and get that lock for you?" She hoped he wasn't trying to steal the machine. It looked as though his life might already be rough enough without adding theft to the mix.

He shook his head once, then reluctantly changed it to a nod. When he got up to give her room she noticed his threadbare sneakers. She gave him a reassuring smile and picked up the rusty lock. That was no doubt half the problem; the mechanism needed oiling. She was relieved to see that he'd used the right combination though. An experimental tug or two later proved her theory. Becky reached into her open bag and searched until she found the small tube of Vaseline she kept for chapped lips. Tommy looked anxious and confused when she handed him the ointment.

"Buddy, I need your help." She wiggled the lock. "I need you to rub some of that lotion onto the lock as I pull. Hopefully we'll get a little bit inside and it'll loosen the mechanism, how does that sound?"

Becky waited while he considered her idea. He finally nodded hesitantly.

"Don't worry," she smiled. "We'll get this." She positioned the lock between them. "Okay, partner, now."

He opened the tube and carefully squeezed it over the lock.

"That's great, Tommy. Now rub it in for me." She kept up a push-pull on either side of the lock until gradually it loosened and finally popped open.

His eyes widened with delight. "You did it," he said, his voice filled with awe.

Rebecca grinned, impressed it actually worked. "No, *we* did it," she said and impulsively leaned over to give him a hug.

He held himself stiff for a moment, then his arms wrapped her middle and squeezed the heck out of her. Warmed by a sudden burst of affection, she dropped a light peck on the top of his head.

A rough tug yanked the boy out of her arms.

"I told you to get yer damn bike and git yerself back home, boy."

Rebecca gasped, startled. A brutish man stood, legs astride, in front of them aiming a malevolent glare toward Tommy. His bullish face sported a bulbous nose lined with ugly red veins and lank, greasy hair. It didn't take much to guess that he spent a good portion of his time on the end of a bottle.

His hand twisted in the scruff of Tommy's jacket, and he gave it a shake. Instant tears sprang to the poor kid's eyes.

"There's no need to be rough," she snapped and reached down to lift her bag from the ground. "I asked him to help me out for a couple of minutes." She studiously ignored his start of surprise. "Is that a problem, Mr.?" She damn sure wanted this joker's name. Jack would be interested to hear how he was treating a little boy.

The guy snorted. "You think I'm an idiot, lady?"

He shoved Tommy toward his bike, almost knocking him off his feet. "Git goin', I'll be right behind ya."

Tommy gave her a helpless glance then yanked his bike out of the rack, threw a leg over the cracked seat, and peddled away as though his life depended on it.

The man moved into her personal space. Rebecca held her ground but her heart was thrashing its way up her throat.

He lifted cigarette stained fingertips and ran them up and down the strap of her purse. "You don't want to mess with me, lady. Just forget today ever happened, you got it?"

Becky swayed, more scared than she'd ever been in her life. She opened her mouth to answer she didn't know what, when a familiar, and at the moment welcoming, voice spoke from over her shoulder.

"Hey, Becky, there you are." Mitch's big body cast a looming shadow over the man in front of her. He took a hasty step back.

Mitch wrapped a muscular arm in a short-sleeved shirt around her waist and tugged her close. Rebecca glanced up to tell him to lay off and cringed at the stony expression at odds with his jovial tone.

"You have a problem with my *wife*, mister, you take it up with me." He stared the other man down, totally ignoring her gasp of outrage. "Got it?" His choice of words made it clear he'd heard at least the end of the conversation.

The man swore and spat on the ground between them—*ew*—then turned and stomped off to a faded red pickup sitting near the school fence.

The engine roared, sending up a blast of blue smoke. He left behind the smell of burnt gas and an uncomfortable silence.

She twisted out of Mitch's hold and fisted her hands on her hips.

"Husband? You're about five years too late to be making that claim, Mitchell Taylor."

Chapter 2

Mitch tracked the departing truck until it disappeared from sight. There was something familiar about that guy…

"Did you hear me?" Becky demanded.

His lips quirked at her impatient tone. Damn, it was easy to get her dander up. He thought how much fun it would be to get her all worked up just so they could have make-up sex. His body hardened, on board with the idea in two seconds flat. *Pathetic, man, you're so pathetic.*

A floppy garden hat shaded her face and matched the hobo handbag she was digging through. She glanced up and her eyes matched the sky for their crystalline brilliance.

Mitch cocked his head toward the road. "What was that about?"

She followed his gaze, visibly shuddered, then squared her shoulders. "Nothing I can't handle." She lifted her chin and he wanted to kiss her. "I'm good at taking care of myself."

Yeah, he knew that.

"I never doubted you could, sweetheart."

A slim hand rose to hold him off. "Stop it," she demanded.

She hesitated, then slipped past him to get her bike. "I have to go. I need to stop by the sheriff's office."

Jealousy flared. Mitch cursed under his breath.

She glanced back. "Pardon me?"

He bit the inside of his lip, warning himself to keep it cool. "I just asked if you wanted me to see Jack so you could go ahead with your day."

A group of pint-sized kids rushed past, pushing and shoving each other in fun.

"See you next week, Miss Sorenson," they called.

She smiled and tugged her bike free of the rack. "Have a good weekend," she answered to their backs. "Did you remember your homework?"

"Yes," they shouted, laughing amongst themselves.

Rebecca placed her purse in the front basket decorated with a large plastic daisy and lifted a shapely leg over the center bar before turning her gaze on him.

"Thanks, but I wanted to speak to Jack for a moment anyway, I'll go." Her butt slid onto the seat, tightening the material of her skirt along her thigh.

He swallowed back the harsh words that threatened to escape, instead answering with a simple nod.

"You never told me why you were here," she said.

No, he hadn't. He nodded over his shoulder, his gaze on her. "Just meeting a friend."

Something flickered behind her eyes. She searched the grounds behind him, then gave him the saddest imitation of a smile he'd ever seen.

"I better go. It was good seeing you, Mitch." She didn't wait for his reply, but pushed off and peddled down the lane until she was out of sight.

"Yeah, you too," he murmured.

* * *

Rebecca kept a steady pace even though everything inside screamed to get away as fast as she could. Her heart beat like a captured bird frantic to escape the walls of her chest. She could barely keep a grip on the handlebars her hands were so sweaty.

Seeing Mitch again had overshadowed the unpleasant encounter with the stranger and her worry for little Tommy. It was months since she'd run into him, ever since Katy had been attacked last fall behind Grace's diner.

He looked good.

His hair was a little longer, but still the same rich gingerbread color she'd loved. His athlete's body had filled out, was more mature now. He'd lost the awkwardness of youth and become a virile, handsome man.

Too handsome for her peace of mind.

A horn honked, scaring the heck out of her. The woman drove past, shaking her head at Becky's stupidity for crossing over the bike lane line.

A timely warning.

Her life was on track, she didn't need to go screwing it up again. Especially over Mitch Taylor.

She signaled a left turn, checked over her shoulder for traffic, and swung onto Elm Street. A couple more blocks and she reached her destination. The sheriff's office looked inviting with the sun warming its red brick façade. Laurel's car still sat in its spot in the receptionist's stall. Rebecca sighed, relieved she hadn't missed her ride. She parked her bike, locked it up, and hurried inside.

Laurel glanced up and broke into a welcoming smile.

"You made it, I was starting to worry." She stood to open the pass-through countertop and let Becky in, wrapping her in a rose-scented hug.

"Sorry, I'm late." Becky met her friend's curious gaze. "I'll tell you all about it on the way there, but first I need to talk to that sexy new husband of yours."

Laurel's cheeks flushed and her eyes sparkled with love. Becky was happy for her. And just think, if her mother hadn't decided to take that long overdue holiday Laurel wouldn't have moved here, taken the job, and been swept off her feet by Jack Garrett.

Sometimes fate worked in mysterious ways.

"Sure, c'mon, he's in his office." Laurel swiveled on four-inch heels—Becky had serious shoe envy—and led the way across the bull-pen. Rebecca smiled and nodded at the men she knew. Deputy Randolph, whose wife was a good friend of her mother's. Sid Carmichael, a longtime veteran of the force. And lastly, Norm Walters.

"Rebecca." Norm hurried to stand, his chair banging against the desk behind him with a loud clang. He cleared his throat and doffed his hat. "How've you been?"

This isn't awkward or anything.

"I'm good, Norm, thanks. How are you doing?" As soon as the words were out, she winced. *Nice job, Einstein.*

She'd gone out with him a few times and had a lot of fun until he started to get serious and she had to call it quits with the ol' 'it's not you, it's me' line, which was just lame even if it was the truth. There had to be something wrong with a woman who had an attractive, nice guy interested and then shut him down just because of a lunch with her no-good ex-husband who she could not get out of her mind.

Norm swept a hand through his wavy dark hair, the muscles in his arms bulging under his uniform.

"Look, Rebecca…"

A door opened a few feet away and Jack stepped out, his face softening when he caught sight of Laurel.

Relieved, Becky laughed, cringing at the higher than normal tone, and smirked at her friend. "You'd think you guys were still newly-weds, when you've already been married what… three months?"

Laurel tapped Becky's shoulder, her gaze fixed on her approaching spouse. "Two months and ten days, as you well know."

That she did. Between Katy and Laurel, and now, Annie, she'd amassed a nice collection of bridesmaid's gowns.

Jack gave Becky a passing glance then settled on his wife. He leaned down, gave Laurel a lingering kiss and whispered something naughty in her ear, going by the hot flush that stained her cheeks.

"Jack, we're not alone," she warned, even as she stepped into his open arms.

He shared an amused glance with Norm before eyeing Becky. "I noticed, my love. What can we do for you, Rebecca?"

Now that she had an audience, Becky wasn't sure how to start.

"I had a problem at the school today." She nervously plucked at the strap of her handbag. "There was this boy, maybe eight or nine years old. I ran into him at the bike rack. He was attempting to unlock an old bike."

"You're thinking he was trying to steal it?" Norm asked.

She shook her head and stuffed a stray lock of hair behind her ear. "No, I don't believe so. He knew the right combination, the lock was just giving him trouble."

"Okay," Jack said, "well, thanks for letting us know." He looked at Norm who shrugged.

Becky sighed. Great, now they thought she was a nitwit. "There's more. A man showed up and told the boy to get home but he wasn't very nice about it. I'm worried. If Mitch Taylor hadn't been there…"

Norm stiffened while Laurel shot her an *I want the details* grin.

Great. Mitch wasn't even in the building and he was causing complications.

Chapter 3

Tommy cried all the way home. Not great hiccupping sobs like he'd done in the past when they'd first arrived at his uncle's house and realized they were worse off now than when their parents died. No, these tears were silent. A steady stream that ran down his face and dripped unheeded off his chin. Tears of despair, of a childhood lost, of faded dreams.

Just for a moment today with that pretty schoolteacher he'd felt something close to peace. Her scent when she'd held him in her arms reminded him of his mom and he hadn't wanted to let go. But then his uncle had shown up.

He reached the edge of town and looked for the overgrown drive. A broken down gray wooden fence and a lopsided *Keep Out* sign pointed the way to the old cabin hidden amongst tall spruce trees. The dirt lane was rutted so bad it tossed his bike from side to side but he refused to walk; his uncle had warned them there were snakes in the grass just waiting for little boys. Tommy wasn't taking any chances.

He pulled up next to the sagging porch and slowly laid his bike on its side, listening for his brother. A soft humming led him to the corner of the building. Jasper sat in the dirt, his scrawny bare back bent over a little toy truck he was using to make roads with in the sand. Tommy sighed his relief, no new marks that he could see. He'd gotten here in time then.

"Hey, brother, whatcha doin'?" He let Jasper know he was there before moving forward.

Jasper jumped up, ready to flee, then realized who'd spoken and cracked a mile wide smile. "Tommy, Tommy you're back." He ran and wrapped his arms around his brother and Tommy frowned at how thin they were.

"Did you eat the food I hid for you?" he demanded.

Jasper shrugged, his chin digging a hole in Tommy's chest. "I wasn't very hungry," he mumbled.

Tommy frowned and set him back so he could look him in the eye. "Jas, you gotta eat. We ain't ever gonna get outta here if you ain't strong enough to run."

Jasper's eyes lit with hope. "Can we go now? Can we, huh?"

Tommy cursed his big mouth. Why'd he go and say anything? "No. We can't go until we have a plan." Jasper's lips wobbled and Tommy changed the subject. "Show me the roads you've been building."

It worked, for now. Jasper trotted over and sprawled out on his belly, reaching for the little blue car he'd been playing with. "Wait 'til you see this. I made a hill and my car flies," he said, his voice filled with excitement.

Tommy followed more slowly, his mind on that nice teacher. Why couldn't someone like her have taken them in? He missed his mom so bad and yet sometimes he got scared because he couldn't quite picture her in his head anymore. The teacher reminded him of her though. She smelled good too and had a pretty dress. His mom always wore nice clothes; she said she liked to look pretty for her boys. Man, he missed her. She'd know what to do right now because he sure didn't. The only thing he did know for certain was that he'd promised to take care of his brother and he darn sure was going to.

The rumble of a vehicle coming up the drive had both boys scrambling for cover. A ratty blue tarp hanging over a pile of scrap metal nearby did the job, though it was a tight fit. Their uncle had warned them often enough to keep outta sight of strangers.

"Who is it?" Jasper asked, his voice squeaky with a mix of fear and excitement.

"Shh, we'll know soon enough," Tommy whispered. "Just keep quiet, okay?"

The rattle as the engine shut down told him who it was even before the tinny door slammed shut and his uncle stomped around the corner looking like the axeman from Snow White.

"Where the hell are you hiding, you stupid little shits?" he roared. His heavy work boots kicked up tufts of dust as he circled the yard in search of them.

He glanced at Jasper's toy car, reached down, picked it up, and sent it flying into the bushes.

Jasper whimpered but thankfully held silent, his body vibrating so hard the tarp rattled. Tommy jerked him away, pulling him up against his own shaking body. He was so scared he needed to pee.

"You come on out of there or your stupid ass brother is going to pay the price." The edge of the tarp lifted and a hand reached in and latched onto Tommy's arm in a death grip. Jasper's eyes grew big as pie plates and welled up with tears. Tommy cried out in pain but shook his head viciously at his brother, warning him to keep quiet and stay still.

And then he was yanked out and thrown to the ground. Uncle Pete stood over him as he lay in the dirt, lips twisted in a snarl that sent shards of fear through Tommy's gut.

"You better explain yourself, boy." He nudged Tommy with his boot. "What did you think you were doing at the schoolhouse today?"

Tommy thought fast. There was no way he was going to tell this man the real reason. He had to come up with something to defuse the anger brewing in his uncle's eyes. He reached into his pocket and reluctantly withdrew the gold chain he'd taken from the teacher lady's purse.

"I was getting you some money, Uncle." A beefy hand reached out and swiped the necklace from his hand. His uncle eyed him suspiciously for a moment before lifting the cross on the chain to the light.

"You aware this is stealing, boy?" He gave the chain a little shake and the cross glinted so bright it practically blinded Tommy.

"I did it just the way you showed me, sir." Tommy lifted himself to his elbows. "She won't know who it was."

Uncle Pete frowned, his brows like bats wings over his eyes. "You better hope the hell not, kid. Your brother doesn't like when you screw up." He laughed, his belly jiggling under the dirty plaid shirt. He turned and strode toward the shack, hollering over his shoulder, "Git in here and make me some grub, I'm hungry after chasing you all over creation."

Tommy waited a few minutes, knowing full well that it was his uncle's routine to go into the house, grab a bottle of booze and flop down on the ugly green sofa for the night. He had time to make sure his brother was okay now.

He pulled back the tarp to let Jasper out, then went searching for the toy car, the last thing Jas had from their mom. A few moments later he found it under the edge of a blackberry bush. Careful to avoid the painful spikes, he managed to retrieve it with only a couple of minor scratches.

"Here you go, buddy, I found it." He turned and offered it to Jasper but his attention was on the house. "Don't worry, I won't let him touch you again." And when his brother looked at him with eyes that knew more than any five-year-old kid outta know about pain, Tommy's gut tightened with a white-hot rage.

He fingered the wallet in his pocket he'd also stolen from the teacher. Soon. Soon he'd have enough to get them far away from here. And they weren't never coming back.

Chapter 4

Rebecca sighed and turned to Jack, the noise of the busy station fading to the background. "Look, I know you think I'm wasting your time but there was something off about that guy, Jack." She met Laurel's sympathetic gaze and attempted a smile but it fell flat. "I'm worried about Tommy."

Jack gave Laurel a peck on the lips before letting his arms drop away. "Okay, let's get a statement and then we'll take it from there, fair enough?"

Rebecca nodded, relieved.

He waved her toward his office. She squeezed Laurel's hand and then slipped between the men, aware that Norm was less than pleased that Jack was going to handle this himself.

She took a place on the edge of a wooden chair and waited for the sheriff to close the door and join her across the man-sized desk. Jack's chair creaked beneath his weight as he rolled it forward and reached for a neat stack of forms beside a geriatric computer.

"Shouldn't you upgrade that thing one day?" Laurel had told her about his reluctance to join the twenty-first century but Becky hadn't taken her seriously.

He patted the clunky top of the monitor affectionately. "Why fix it, if it ain't broke?" He pulled a pink pen from his pocket, and grimaced when she smirked. "Laurel gave me this as a reminder of the first time we met."

Oh, she'd heard. Laurel liked to share with almost anyone who'd listen how smitten she'd been the first time she laid eyes on the handsome sheriff— and how he'd almost stolen her favorite pen.

"What can you tell me about the kid?" He waited, pen poised over legal looking papers and Rebecca suddenly realized she might be jumping to conclusions and causing unnecessary difficulty for the boy.

"Well, he seemed kind of shy, at least to start with." She reached into her bag, searching for the chain she always fingered when she was nervous or upset. It wasn't in the side pocket where she normally kept it for safety. What the heck? Giving up on subtlety she ducked her head and began to paw through the bag and that's when she noticed something else missing—her wallet.

"What's wrong?" Jack tapped his pen on the desk and stared at her curiously.

Becky glanced up, met his narrowed gaze, and returned to combing through her purse. *Please, be there. Please, please…*

It wasn't, and if she confessed the loss, Tommy would be in a lot of trouble. She didn't have the heart to do that to a kid who already had two strikes against him. Faking a nonchalance she was far from feeling, Becky withdrew a lipstick and tried to touch up her lips without trembling noticeably. The wallet was bad, but at least those items could be replaced—the chain on the other hand…

Jack leaned back in his seat and frowned. "What's this really about, Rebecca?"

She rotated the bottom of the tube until the lipstick disappeared, carefully capped the top and stowed it away before meeting Jack's gaze.

"I've met men like that guy who bothered Tommy before. They aren't nice men, Jack." She tucked a strand of hair behind her ear and fingered the scar on her neck. "They take pleasure in abusing those weaker than themselves."

Jack contemplated the ceiling for a long moment, then sat up, and the sympathy lighting his dark brown eyes warmed her heart even as it embarrassed her.

"Okay, let's say you're right. We can start an investigation on him and see who he is and what he's been up to. How's that sound?"

Becky sighed her relief. "Thanks, Jack."

* * *

Mitch couldn't get his mind off his ex-wife. He needed to get moving and catch up to Kyle Fowler, who was at the school waiting to pick up a kid as a favor to his twin sister, Katy. She was planning a bachelorette party for the child's mother, while Kyle and the new groom-to-be, Jared Martin, were in charge of the kidlets.

Kyle was only in town for a short visit so Mitch had to meet him when he could, even if that meant hanging out in an elementary school yard. And running into the one woman he wanted to avoid. Rebecca Sorenson Taylor. That's still how he thought of her, though the ink hadn't even dried on the separation papers before she'd changed her name back.

Normally it wasn't a problem to stay out of her way, they didn't exactly move in the same social orbit. He was steel-toed boots and beer at Duke's Bar while she was pretty dresses and fancy meals at La Lune—the two didn't match. He still wasn't quite sure how they'd ended up hitched in the first place.

Okay, that was a lie.

He'd taken a trip to Vegas to try and forget about the fact that his career as a football star was in the toilet and his life was running a close second. He'd been working on getting drunk in a bar off the strip when she'd strolled into the lounge wearing a little black dress designed to drive a man crazy. Mitch knew who she was right away, he remembered her from school, so he'd waved her over and found out she was in town for a teacher's convention and, bless his luck, had lost track of her group. They'd ended up spending the most amazing night of his life together. By the time he got up the next morning he'd been married and she'd been gone.

He'd wasted his last hours in the city trying to find her, then hopped an early flight home. A few days later the separation papers arrived and he'd known it was just a dream. Love didn't happen at first sight. Lust, hell, yeah. But love… that was something poets wrote about, it wasn't reality.

Since then they'd made a career out of avoiding each other, and in a town of only seven thousand people that wasn't always easy. He'd run into her more than once when one or the other of them were out on a date with someone else. Talk about your soap opera moments. They should just file for divorce and end this insanity, but he couldn't bring himself to make it final.

"You turning on the old Taylor charm again, bro?" Kyle joined him near the bike rack, a little boy with reddish hair and a freckled face lagging close behind.

Mitch forced a laugh and smiled down at the kid. "You must be Chris. I've been friends with your dad for a long time."

Chris considered him from serious green eyes. "Are you from the navy too?"

Mitch shook his head and crouched to meet Chris's gaze. "No. Your dad was pretty brave to do what he did, like Uncle Kyle here." He glanced up to see if Kyle was listening. He was. "They both did their duty, but now it's time they enjoy their lives. Your dad told me how excited he is to make you guys part of his family."

Chris looked up at Kyle and then nodded his understanding. "Yes, sir, my mom's real happy too."

Mitch's heart gave a painful tug. This could easily be his story, getting to know a son he had no knowledge of until years later. Kudos to Jared and Annie for solving their issues to give this little boy the family he deserved. He rose and shrugged off the envy he felt. At least Jared wasn't alone anymore.

"How about some ice cream?" There weren't very many problems that couldn't be solved over a heaping dish of vanilla ice cream covered in chocolate sauce and sprinkles.

Chris and Kyle both wore identical grins and after a resounding high-five they were off, Mitch in his welding truck, while Kyle drove a shiny black jeep. They pulled up at The Soda Shoppe and strolled to the front door behind a group of chattering teen girls whose laughter suited the warm and sunny weather.

Mitch held the door and smiled at a familiar looking girl as she passed through the opening. He was surprised when Chris ran ahead and tugged on her hand.

"Tina," he shouted. "I'm getting some ice cream."

The girl stopped and smiled down at the boy. "Hey, Chris, I didn't see you. Are you here with your mom?" She searched the room, briefly meeting Mitch's gaze before glancing away.

"No." Chris waved his hand at them. "I'm with my dad's friends. My mom's going to a party." The touch of pride in his voice when he mentioned his dad put a lump in Mitch's throat.

"I'm going to get in line," Kyle said. "You got him?"

Mitch nodded. He strode over to introduce himself and realized why she seemed familiar; she was Jack's daughter.

There'd been a time when he and Jack Garrett had done damn near everything from hockey practice, homework, and hanging out, to chasing women, drinking, and football, together. And then April Montgomery came into their lives and nothing was ever the same. Tina had her face and the promise of her mother's killer body, but it was Jack's friendly brown eyes smiling innocently at him right now.

"Hi, Mr. Taylor. My dad's told me a lot about you," she said, her gaze curious as it rested on him.

So Jack talked about him, did he? Interesting.

"Your father and I go way back," he said, and frowned when some boys jostled her as they hurried past to grab a table. "I better let you go, this place looks pretty busy."

Her smile shy, she nodded and ruffled Chris's hair. "I'll see you at the shop, sport." And then she was gone in a cloud of sweet-smelling perfume and long blonde hair. Jack was going to have his hands full in a couple more years.

"She works for my mom," Chris offered in the silence, his gaze pensive as he watched her flirting with the boys.

Mitch well remembered his first crush so he diverted the kid's attention. "Looks like Kyle's ordering without us, we better get up there." He turned, ushering the kid ahead of him and came face to face with Jack.

Kyle better be grabbing him a double scoop.

Chapter 5

Mitch nodded a passing acknowledgement, and placed his hand on Chris's shoulder to guide him along. There'd been too much water under the bridge for either him or Jack to ever be comfortable in one another's company. And sadly, it was all due to a stupid misunderstanding.

"Mitch, I need a word." Jack halted him in his tracks. "You got a minute?"

Mitch wasn't sure what this was about but he didn't plan on being the afternoon's entertainment either. They were already drawing attention.

"Yeah, sure, Chief. Just let me get my buddy here settled and I'll meet you out front."

Jack nodded and turned away to greet his daughter. His big body dwarfed hers even though she was fairly tall for her age. Mitch placed her at around fifteen or sixteen. Funny, how much time had passed by without him realizing it. She'd been around young

Chris's age when her mother left town. Dark days those were. That woman had done her level best to destroy anyone in her path. Even though it cost him his career and his best friend, Mitch celebrated the day April Montgomery left Tidal Falls.

Chris's squirming body under his hand reminded him of what he was supposed to be doing. A quick search found Kyle surrounded by a group of too-young-for-him girls all vying for his attention. And he was soaking it up, a come-to-papa smile on his lips.

"There he is, kid. Let's go catch up to our ice cream before he gives it away."

Kyle shrugged when they drew near, laughter turning his eyes a clover green. "'Bout time. I thought you said you were buying."

Mitch pretended to check his pocket. "Sorry, mate, next time." He grinned, unrepentant, and snagged the smallest and the biggest dishes from the counter. "Here you go, kid."

Chris's eyes grew wide at the sight of his treat topped with chocolate and candy pieces. "Wow, my mom never lets me have this much."

Kyle's brows lowered. He reached for the bowl but Chris yanked it away. "Hey."

"Well, if you're going to get into trouble…"

Chris shoved a heaping spoonful into his mouth and the girls giggled.

"He's cute."

"Aw."

"My brother's just like that."

"Hey look, there's Tony Secora." A young teen with a mouth full of braces, pointed excitedly toward some newcomers. And just like that Kyle became yesterday's news as they took off in hope of catching the jock's attention.

"You know you're old when…" Mitch joked.

"A bunch of simpering girls gives you a headache," Kyle finished, and both men grinned.

"What's so funny?" Chris wanted to know, glancing back and forth between them, ice cream dripping down his chin.

Mitch grabbed a napkin and gave him a swipe. "You'll know when you get to be dinosaurs like us, kid. Now we're all roar and no action."

"Speak for yourself, *Dino*," Kyle mumbled around a scoop of banana and whipped cream. He lifted a maraschino cherry by its stem and deposited it on the lopsided mountain in Chris's bowl.

Mitch noticed Jack leaving and his mood sank. What the hell did the sheriff want, unless this had something to do with the school incident earlier today?

His mouth tightened. If Becky was in trouble he wanted to know about it. The ice cream felt like it was curdling in his gut and he pushed the half-full bowl away.

Kyle eyed it and then him. "Not your flavor, or what?"

Mitch snorted. "How can you go wrong with vanilla?" He pressed away from the counter. "I'm just going to step outside for a minute—be right back."

Kyle's gaze followed Jack's departing back. He frowned. "You sure, man?"

Mitch shrugged. "He wants to talk."

Kyle cursed under his breath. Chris's head swiveled back and forth like a bobble-head as he tried to keep up with the conversation.

"I'm here if you need me, dude, but don't hurt his pretty face. He's family now," Kyle warned.

Mitch gave Chris a fist bump and started back through the ever-growing crowd. Now that school was out it seemed as though every teen in town was here. Kyle didn't need to worry, he and Jack had come to an understanding long ago. If the two of them were going to remain in Tidal Falls—and they were—it was necessary. They'd even sat at the same table for Kyle's twin sister's wedding to Jack's brother, Ty, last fall. And if the occasional barb passed between the two men, it was still very civilized. No spilled drinks or anything. He figured he'd done pretty fricken good considering Jack's date for the night was none other than Rebecca. His Becky.

The door slammed open with more force than he intended, banging against the stopper and rattling the glass. Great, might as well announce his antagonism to the world and get it over with.

Jack stood a few feet away, his face impassive. His arms were crossed over his chest and his hat was tipped back on his head in a show of two-buds-havin'-a-chat. Nothing to see here.

"Tough day?"

Mitch hated that cool exterior, and itched to ruffle the man's composure. Instead, he shrugged and dug a toothpick out of his pocket. The sharp bite of the peppermint-flavored stick calmed his temper before he got himself in shit. He needed to remember this was the sheriff, not his nemesis.

"It was alright. What's up, Sheriff?"

Jack nodded toward the parking lot where his vintage flat black 'stang sat at the far end, away from possible fender-benders. "Let's go over there where we won't be overheard."

Those words did nothing to ease Mitch's anxiety, but he played nice and strolled through the mixture of four-by's and cruisers kids preferred to drive these days. He came to a stop near the Mustang's back fender.

"Okay, we're here. What's going on?"

Jack took his hat off and rubbed a hand through his short nut-brown hair before replacing the ivory Stetson on his head.

"I heard you were at Cascade Elementary today."

Mitch stiffened. "Yeah. Is it against the law?"

Jack kicked at a few loose rocks, sending them skittering across the top of the pavement. "Don't be an ass, Taylor. I only mentioned it because Rebecca Sorenson dropped by the office today and she was understandably upset over an incident I believe you were a witness to, am I right?"

Mitch propped a hip on the back fender and ignored Jack's lowered brows. "Yeah, I was there. She tried to help a kid and ended up getting reamed out by some old drunk for her trouble."

"Did you get a good look at either one?" Jack tapped his shirt pocket and pulled out a coiled notepad and a girly looking pink pen.

Mitch smirked. "Nice pen." Then he straightened and got serious. "The kid had dark wavy hair, brown eyes, about four foot tall, and wore threadbare clothes on a too-skinny frame." He waited for Jack to jot down the information. "The guy acted like a guardian or something. He stunk of booze and B.O., and drove a faded red pickup that's seen better days." Again he waited for Jack to finish writing before he dropped his bombshell.

"I've been thinking about it all afternoon and I think I know who that guy is."

"Well?" Jack asked pink pen poised.

"I'm almost positive it's your brother-in-law, Jack."

Chapter 6

The entire time Rebecca, Laurel, and Katy were setting up for the evening's events, Becky couldn't get the afternoon out of her mind. She laughed and joked with the caterers and teased Laurel on her obsession with a certain burly sheriff, but continually replayed the abject fear on Tommy's face when he'd been manhandled by that creep. She should have done something more to control the situation. It worried her what might have happened after Tommy got home. The signs of abuse, at least mental if not physical, had been there and she'd let him go. But it had happened so fast there'd been no real response time until it was too late.

She sighed and rearranged the cutlery for at least the tenth time. Hopefully Jack would do as he said and look into the child's home-care condition for her.

"You're going to wear the silver right off that knife soon," Laurel said from behind her shoulder.

Becky smiled and set the piece down before turning to her friend. "Oh, you look gorgeous." Laurel had switched from her workday clothes to a shell pink sequined party dress that should have clashed wildly with her red-gold hair and fair complexion. Instead, it brought her to vivid, runway model perfection.

Laurel blushed and ran nervous pink-tipped nails down her hips. "Do you think it's too much? I know this is Annie's night, but I saw this dress and fell in love."

Rebecca shook her head and grabbed her friend's hands. "You look amazing. Jack's not going to know what hit him." The two shared a smile. "Don't worry about Annie. If I know her, she's going to show up in something incredible and knock Jared flat on his butt."

Laurel laughed and Becky was pleased to see the doubt vanish from her eyes. They'd clicked right from the moment they met in college. Laurel had come to town just before Christmas for a temporary job and ended up engaged to the sheriff. Becky was happy for them. No one deserved a second chance more than Jack did. He was everything a father should be for Tina. The whole town had stood behind him after the accident and the subsequent loss of his football career.

"Where's Katy?" Laurel glanced around the newly decorated backroom of Duke's Bar.

"She just went to check on the kitchen."

It was a huge stress-reliever to arrange flowers and lay out tablecloths after the day from hell she'd just endured. Duke had offered the space to them pro bono and it worked out perfectly for their plans. The attached Rendezvous Hotel hosted a well-organized kitchen willing to cater the event, there were even rooms available for those who over-imbibed. The decorating had gone smoothly and Duke agreed to supply the alcohol and entertainment.

Becky glanced down at her own black velvet dress. Mitch would have liked it; he was a very tactile man. The mink-like texture would appeal to him. A ghostly sensation of calloused fingers feathered across her torso and made her shiver. Damn him. Five years later and he still occupied way too many of her thoughts. After this wedding chaos with Annie was finished she needed to find a lawyer and quietly end their marriage. It was time to move on.

She took a big gulp of the white Zinfandel she'd been sipping on for the past couple hours and promptly choked. Coughing and sputtering, she felt like an idiot as she waved away Laurel's concerned attempt to pat her back. By the time it settled her eyes were teary and her face burned with embarrassment.

"Classy, hey?" She used a mauve monogrammed napkin to dry her lips leaving a blot of bright red lipstick behind.

Katy entered from the far set of doors before Laurel could comment, her lemon slip dress glowing under the track lighting. "Okay, the kitchen's ready. I think we have us a party, girlfriends." When she drew closer she noticed the tears and her brow creased with concern. "What's going on? What did I miss?"

"Just me not able to hold my liquor, no worries." Becky hurried to assure her best friend. Tonight was about having a good time, dammit, and no six-foot pain in the ass was going to ruin it for her.

Katy smiled, relieved, and lifted her flute in a toast. "To love, ladies."

They clinked glasses and took a sip just as the first guests began to arrive. To love, wherever it may be.

* * *

Mitch straightened his tie for what felt like the hundredth time and gazed around the crowd of partygoers. He wasn't sure what drove him to come here tonight. His plan had been to hang with Kyle and the kids, but when asked he'd jumped on Jared's invitation like a dirty shirt. Speaking of which… He looked down and made sure his tie covered the small grease stain on his dress shirt.

This so wasn't his kind of thing.

He should just go. It wasn't like he'd be welcomed anyway. These were Jack's friends, Jack's family. And besides, this night was for Jared and Annie. They didn't need him around causing dissent.

He'd just turned to make his way back to the bar when a hand clapped him on the back.

"Mitch Taylor, it's been a long, long time, son."

Mitch swallowed hard and swung around. Jack's grandfather stood before him, older, stooped, but with the same kind eyes and warm smile he'd always had for his grandkid's friends.

"Mr. Garrett. It's great to see you, sir." He stuck out a hand and was instead engulfed in a surprisingly strong man-hug.

"No need to stand on formality with me, young man. I've known you too damn long for that." Mr. Garrett leaned back but kept hold of his shoulders in a firm grip. "Neil, call me Neil." He waited until Mitch nodded before letting him go. "Now, what say you and I head over to the bar and get ourselves a drink?" He winked and nodded behind him to the server surrounded by guests in the corner of the room.

Without waiting for a reply, the elder Garrett began to make his way through the crush of people.

Mitch sighed. He couldn't leave now, someone might plow the old man over by accident. He had to follow.

"Mitch, glad you could make it." Neil's sister, Tess Garrett smiled as she leaned in and kissed her brother's cheek. "Neil, don't forget you owe me a dance."

Neil grumbled but it was easy to see the affection between the siblings. As if on cue, the overhead lights dimmed and a four-piece band that had been setting up on stage strummed a few preliminary chords.

All eyes turned to the dance floor, the spotlight picking out a vision in gold lame as Annie glided onto the floor. But Mitch couldn't take his gaze off the stunning beauty holding her hand. Rebecca wore a heart-stopping, thigh-hugging, breath-stealing dress that made him want to rip out every guy's eyes from their skulls. And that was before she laughingly turned to dance with her friend and made his mouth run dry. There must have been a shortage of velvet material because there was no damn back on that thing. He could almost see down to the top of her ass for crying out loud. How the hell did it stay up?

He was on the move before the opening notes died away, peeling his dinner jacket off his shoulders as he went. His temperature rose with every step. What was she thinking? A dress like that meant one thing only. If she wanted sex then it was damn well going to be with him and no one else. She was his wife. Maybe it was about time he reminded her of that fact.

Annie looked startled when she caught sight of him stomping towards them. Then her eyes lit with satisfaction and she performed a twirl worthy of a score of ten to bring Becky's gaze around to him. She stumbled to a halt, a hand going defensively to her breast.

"Mitch, what are you doing here?" she hissed.

More than aware he was making a spectacle of himself, he stepped forward and threw his coat around her shoulders. Holding the ends together under her chin, he tipped her wide-eyed gaze to his and stole Tess's line. "I think you owe me a dance."

Her cornflower blue eyes flickered with anger and something else—despair? Before he had time to ponder the significance she turned away and apologized to Annie. "Do you mind?"

Annie shot him a *you-better-treat-her-right* warning glare over Becky's head before giving a reassuring smile to her friend. "Of course not. You go ahead. Besides," she nodded to the handsome man pushing his way through the crowd, "I think our party is officially crashed." She didn't seem too upset by that as Jared swept her up in a searing kiss that turned up the temperature in the room by several degrees.

With a last wistful look at the happy couple, Becky turned to Mitch and the contrast in her expression was like a slam to the gut.

"Shall we?" she said, her tone anything but welcoming.

Some perverse demon riding his shoulder prodded him to force her into admitting their relationship to her friends. The peace-making angel on the other side whispered dire warnings in his ear.

He'd only make things worse. She'd never forgive him. He'd lose her forever.

Mitch brushed them both away and forged his own path. He nudged a stray black curl behind her ear, satisfaction curling like warm smoke between them as he registered her involuntary reaction.

"Oh yes, sweetheart, we shall." And they both knew he wasn't talking about the dancing.

Chapter 7

Rebecca was in Hell.

What other explanation could there be for the reappearance of Mitch in her life when she'd worked so diligently to avoid him for the best part of eighteen hundred and eighteen days—not that she was counting.

The divorce papers sitting on the desk at home were burning a hole through her brain, making her ache with things she dared not admit.

He looked amazing, by far the handsomest man in a room full of fine-looking men. His white dress shirt emphasized the breadth of those impossibly wide shoulders, honed to steel by years of honest manual labor. But then she'd always admired that about him. When his football career had come to an abrupt end he could have turned to a bottle and no one would have faulted him for it. Instead he picked himself up, went to a community college, got his welding ticket, and opened a business. Now his work was often sought after from all over the state and his shop had grown from a backyard garage to a fully equipped warehouse on a prime piece of Tidal Falls land. Mitch Taylor was a local success story.

He grasped her hand and she reluctantly followed his lead across a floor now packed with swaying bodies. He didn't stop until they reached a shadowed alcove off to one side of the stage. When he turned and held out his arms she stepped forward like a lamb, letting his jacket drop onto a nearby chair. The moment his arms wrapped around her and his calloused fingers found the bare skin of her lower back, Becky knew she was in trouble.

Her startled gaze rushed upward and tangled in the molten heat of his amber eyes. The light and shadows created by their surroundings turned his face lean and mysterious and oh-so-hypnotic. Someone bumped into them but she barely noticed, she was so caught up in his aura. It had been like this before—in Las Vegas.

Rebecca tried to pull away, her heart beating double time, an out-of-sync counterpoint to the drums playing on stage. Mitch simply tugged so that she had to grasp the front of his shirt to keep from falling—not that he would have let her. There were many things about Mitch Taylor that bothered her, but she never doubted his kindness.

He bowed his head and rested his cheek against her temple and his voice rumbled through her soul. "It's just a dance, sweetheart. What are you afraid of?"

Everything.

Him.

Herself.

She gave in and let him win this round. Besides, her body had already betrayed her and snuggled into the protective warmth of his chest.

They were barely moving. Her hips brushing against his hardened thighs left her breathless and aching, not helped by his fingers exploring each curve and valley of her spine like braille.

Her own hands were busy documenting the changes since they'd last known the ridges and planes of a man's chest. They may have been separated but she'd never once given thought to sleeping with anyone else, even if her marriage was little more than a joke.

Disturbed from her sensual fog, Rebecca lifted her head with the intention of ending this farce. But before she could string two words together Mitch's lips lowered to hers. All the lights and sounds became a sparkling kaleidoscope and mixed with the sheer perfection of his mouth.

Oh my...

She could die happy right now, in this moment. That wicked, delicious tongue knew where every nerve was located and how to parry and thrust until Becky was utterly lost. She hung on for dear life, eyes sealed shut to keep the world at bay. Every sense was on fire. Her skin prickled, desperate to know the mastery of his touch. He held her so close she could feel his arousal.

Somehow, that helped. Knowing he was as affected by what was happening as she was made her feel less helpless, more in control.

Her arms roped his neck, keeping his head where she wanted him while her pelvis ground shamelessly against his erection, desperate for some kind of release… until the nearby laughter from a couple of women nearby ripped the blindfold away.

What was she doing?

They'd practically been having sex in the middle of the dance floor for crying out loud. Frantic, she tried to push away, her gaze searching for witnesses, and only minimally relaxing when she realized the room was half dark and no one was looking at them. Mitch refused to let her go, and she growled, "Get your hands off of me."

Slow on the uptake, it took him a moment to switch focus and realize she wasn't on the same page anymore. Hell, she didn't even want to be in the same book.

He loosened his grip and took a step back, hands raised in surrender. "Calm down. What's your problem?"

Seriously?

"You, Mitch Taylor. You're my fricken problem. But not for much longer."

She turned, and with as much dignity as a woman on the edge could summon, she walked off the dance floor and into the blessed darkness.

Chapter 8

Mitch listened to the clanging of the band—or was that his brain?—for a few seconds then started off the dance floor in search of his estranged wife. Enough with this bullshit. He was sick and tired of her walking out on him. They needed to hash this thing between them out one way or the other.

He only hesitated long enough to grab his jacket and take a deep calming breath. Rebecca was driving him crazy. Maybe it would be best if he let her do as she so obviously wanted and divorce him. Then they could continue on with their lives, instead of living in this limbo. The problem was he couldn't picture letting her go. She'd wormed her way under his skin that night in Vegas and he couldn't seem to extricate her.

Mitch punched a hole through the crowd, anxious to find her. He headed in the same general direction she'd taken but stopped when Ty slapped him on the back.

"Hey, glad you could make it."

He shook his friend's hand while searching the crowded room. No sign of her. Where did she disappear to so quickly?

Sighing, he focused on Ty and his new wife, Katy. "How's the theatre working out?" He'd been grateful for the opportunity to update the old Twilight Theatre last fall for Katy and her family. The building was a town landmark and the job had been a bonus for his business.

She beamed up at him, a ray of sunshine with her shiny blonde hair and yellow dress. "It's perfect. Ty and I can't thank you enough. We're getting bookings from as far away as Seattle. They heard of the new multi-level stage and want to try it out. Isn't that great?"

Mitch swallowed his envy as she gazed adoringly at her husband. He craved someone like that to share his successes with. He was damn tired of going back to an empty house at night.

He smiled at Katy's enthusiasm. "You can thank your husband. Those plans of his kicked butt."

"I have more where they came from. We should talk," Ty said, sliding an arm around his wife's trim waist.

Mitch had enjoyed the challenge of making Ty's dream a reality. If he had more ideas of that caliber... "I'm interested. Meet me at the office tomorrow."

"Meet for what?" The unmistakable rumble came from behind and Mitch tensed before twisting to meet Jack's ever-so-friendly scowl. Laurel stood at his side, ravishing as always, her pale pink nails wrapped around his arm.

"Just talking business, bro, no worries." Ty grinned, not in the least intimidated by his older brother. "Good thing I'm a happily married man or I'd be thinking of stealing your wife away tonight. You look amazing, Laurel."

Laurel smiled good-naturedly. "You Garretts are all the same, natural born flirts."

Mitch smirked. Ignoring Jack, he leaned over and bussed first Laurel's cheek, then Katy's. "Fun as this is turning out to be, I need to get going. I'm trying to catch up to someone."

That caught the women's attention.

Damn. Women's intuition was a scary thing.

"She ducked out the back door," Katy said, and grasped his arm. "Don't go unless you mean it, Mitch Taylor. Someone scared her off men a long time ago. She doesn't need you if you're not serious."

He appreciated the warning; they were only trying to protect their friend. Actually Mitch was relieved Rebecca had a strong support network. There was nothing worse than feeling alone in this world. He should know.

"Honey, they have to work out whatever it is for themselves," Ty said, and gave Mitch an awkward shrug.

Mitch smiled and patted Katy's hand. "Don't worry, I promise not to hurt her. I only want what's best for Becky." And if that included him, so much the better.

* * *

Rebecca pushed open the steel exit door and reveled in the cool caress of night air on her flushed body. She'd like to attribute her warmth to the crowded party but knew it had more to do with Mitch and her momentary loss of control. Thank goodness none of her friends had seen them necking like a couple of teenagers or she'd never live it down.

Becky prided herself in being the levelheaded member of their group. She was the one others came to for advice. Ironic really, since she didn't have the foggiest idea what to do with her own love life.

"Well, what do we have here?"

She inhaled a startled gasp as two men came out from the shadows of the building and scared the crap out of her.

The tall, skinny one sneered. "Hello, pretty lady. Did you make a wrong turn?"

She backed up against the door, her head shouting to get the hell out of there.

"I don't want any… any trouble." She pushed, but the door wouldn't budge.

"Hey, ain't you that teacher we saw this afternoon?" The other man moved closer to stare at her through blurry eyes and Becky's heart crammed into her throat. It was Tommy's guardian, or whoever he was. This wasn't good, not good at all.

"Look, you guys can go back to whatever you were doing." She really didn't want to know. "I have a friend joining me right away. He wouldn't like it if you bothered me."

"Ooh, tough talk, teach. Except I don't see anybody out here except us chickens," Tommy's guardian cackled. Then the smile slowly faded and something much darker took its place. "I think maybe I should be the one to school you a lesson. One on how to mind your own good goddamn business." He grasped her arm and yanked her away from the door so hard she fell against his sour-smelling body. "What do you think of that, Teach?"

Rebecca let out a yelp just before his lips mashed against her teeth. His tongue poked out and tried to force an entry. Becky bit down hard and he jerked back. The next thing she knew she was seeing stars as his fist exploded against the side of her face. She tasted blood and gagged, not sure if it was his or hers. He let go and she fell to her hands and knees, barely registering the scrape of cement breaking skin.

Stunned, she panted through the pain then tried to scramble away but the skinny guy grabbed her hair, tipping her head back while he fought with his zipper. "We're going to have us some fun tonight," he crowed.

Petrified, Becky reached up and frantically tried to free herself from his grip, her breath see-sawing so hard it burned her chest.

A muted clang and then a roar sounded in the distance followed by the sudden release of her hair. Rebecca sank to the ground, the pavement cool against her aching face, and let the tears flow.

Chapter 9

Mitch pushed the steel bar to open the exit doors and peered to see through the rays of light streaming from the hallway. They could use some better illumination back here. Rebecca wouldn't be foolish enough to wander around in the dark, would she?

Something turned his gaze to the far side of the alley and his heart stopped. Time warped. Becky was on the ground with two dark, hulking figures standing over her. One of them had her hair twisted in his fist, yanking her head back viciously.

Mitch saw red.

A growl rose from his chest and he charged them, the urge to kill taking over logical thought. They noticed him at the last moment and attempted to run, casting Rebecca aside like a piece of trash.

That was their first mistake.

The second was assuming he'd let them go.

He caught the guy who had hurt her with a roundhouse jab to the chin, snapping his head backward with a resounding crack. He dropped like a felled tree.

Mitch crouched to make sure Becky was okay. Her sobs twisted his insides into a knot of helpless rage. He brushed a gentle hand down her back to let her know she was safe, and cursed when she recoiled.

Anger rode him hard.

His focus shifted to the asshole cowering against a stack of garbage cans. He pulled his cell from his pocket, rose and stalked the scum, more than ready to pounce if he even breathed wrong.

"Tidal Falls County Sheriff's Office," a competent female voice chirped in his ear.

"I need help. There's been an assault." Mitch hesitated, "You'd better send an ambulance."

"Okay, sir, slow down." The dispatcher became all business. "I need your name and where you are so we can send someone to assist. Are you in any danger?"

Mitch turned to check on the fallen man who had started to groan. "No, but…"

Something slammed his head with the force of a sledgehammer. The blow drove Mitch to his knees. Squinting through a haze of pain he watched the blurry form step carefully around him, throwing the two-by-four aside and hefting his partner to his feet before the pair of them loped off down the alley.

Fuck.

Talk about your rookie mistake. He deserved the splitting headache no doubt heading his way. He felt around on the ground until his hand connected with the cracked body of his cellphone. *Great.*

Giving up on the phone he rose and stumbled back to Rebecca. She lifted her head as he kneeled beside her and Mitch swore a blue streak. Her right eye and cheek had already turned several shades of purple and her lip was split and sore looking.

"Oh, baby," he murmured. He laid a gentle hand against the injury, wishing like hell he could draw the pain into his body.

Rebecca raised her shaking hand in turn and touched his aching forehead with cool fingertips. "You're bleeding."

Mitch ignored that, more interested in making sure they hadn't done anything worse before he arrived on scene. "Did those bastards lay a hand on you?"

Her eyes overflowed. She shook her head. Mitch sighed his relief. He flopped down on his ass and wrapped his arms around her, tucking her up tight against his heart while sirens wailed in the distance.

The exit doors slammed back on their hinges. First Jack—who'd probably received a call from the station—then Ty, Jared, and half the damn town spilled into the alley.

"What the hell, Taylor?" Jack demanded, towering over their prone bodies.

Mitch didn't bother to raise his head from its safe haven against Rebecca's tousled hair, it hurt too damn much. "Hey, chief."

"Give them some room," he yelled, and Mitch scowled as the words reverberated in his brain.

"C'mon, back it up." Then he crouched beside them and Mitch would've smirked at the crack from Jack's knees if he didn't hurt so bad. "What happened, Mitch? Is Rebecca hurt?"

No shit, Dick Tracy.

"Nah, we just decided to take a break. Out here…" He glared at Jack. "In. The. Freaking. Alley." His tone rose with each syllable, but he couldn't help it. The adrenaline had ebbed, leaving him shaking and about to go bonkers. What if he hadn't followed her? Who the fuck were they? Where was that ambulance?

Rebecca lifted her head and the men around them collectively swore.

"Holy shit."

"What the hell happened?"

"Calm down," Becky lisped, her poor lip swollen and discolored. "I'm fine. Mitch showed up before anything worse could happen." She turned her gaze on him. "I guess I owe you. Again."

Mitch's brows lowered. He didn't need her feeling beholden to him. It was sheer good luck that he happened to be in the right place at the right time.

First with that kid's guardian, then... hey, wait a minute. Why hadn't he noticed before?

"It was him, wasn't it? The same asshole that bothered you this afternoon at school." He turned to Jack. "Why haven't you caught him yet? If you did your job, this never would've happened."

Ty stepped forward. "Hey, man, cool it. Whatever it is you're talking about, you know Jack's doing everything he possibly can."

Jack glanced at his brother over his shoulder. "It's okay, Ty. He has reason to be pissed. I'd feel the same way." The deputy's car turned into the alley with the ambulance hot on its tail. The emergency lights flashing on the walls created a surreal image of the scene.

Jack rose and went to meet the car, leaving an uneasy silence in his wake. Mitch nodded to Jared, who reached down and helped Rebecca to her feet. Ty held out a hand to Mitch. He contemplated ignoring him but thought better of it and grabbed on, squeezing his eyes shut against the resulting pain and dizziness at the change in elevation. *Whoa*, might have a bit of a concussion going on. Getting hit in the head with a chunk of wood could do that to a guy.

The ambulance attendants rushed over with medical bags and proceeded to twenty question Becky who was looking worse by the minute. Mitch waved away the one who turned to him. His only concern was to see that Rebecca got the care she needed. A few minutes and a thorough exam later a gurney was brought out against her wishes and she was headed for the hospital.

Mitch followed to the back of the ambulance and watched them load her inside. The female attendant turned to him, her hand on the door, "Are you a family member of the patient?"

How was he supposed to answer that one? Screw it, he intended to ride to the hospital with her and there was only one sure-fire way to make that happen.

"I'm her husband."

Chapter 10

Peter Montgomery was sick and fricken tired of do-gooders getting into his business. It wasn't like they were going to hurt that teacher-lady. They was just havin' a bit of fun with her, that's all. He cursed and yanked Davey into a recessed doorway as a cop car raced past. Just what he needed, the fucking cops on his tail. It didn't matter that his stupid sister's ex was the sheriff. There'd be no help from that quarter.

"Where's that bottle o' whiskey I told you to hold on to?" He held out a shaky hand and frowned, grasping his wrist to hold it steady.

Davey backed up another step and almost tripped over a cement stair. "I dropped it when we ran."

Pete cursed and lunged forward.

"It slipped." Davey covered his head and cowered. "I didn't mean to. C'mon man, take it easy." He felt around in his jacket pockets and pulled out a silver pint flask. "Here, have some of this, it's better anyway. One-eighty proof. I made it myself."

Pete snapped it out of his hand almost before the idiot quit yammering. He twisted the cap off, gave the top a swipe with his coat sleeve, and took an appreciative sniff. Yep, Davey knew how to make some damn fine hooch, that's for sure. The first sip burned its way down his gut like a dragon's breath and he let out a little gasp.

Davey reached for the flask and Pete batted his hands away, glaring. Then he lifted the half-full container to his lips and drank deep, letting it wash the anger and frustration away.

"Hooyah," he wheezed when the carafe was finally drained. He stumbled and lost his balance for a minute, smacking up against the tin-sided building.

"Shh," he said, and then laughed.

Davey stood him up and retrieved his now empty flask, stuffing it into his jacket. "Thanks for sharing, man. C'mon, we better get movin' before the cops show up." He shoved a shoulder under Pete's arm, almost reefing the thing out of its socket.

"Take it easy. I use that once in awhile you know." He guffawed at his own crude joke.

"Yah, man, you're a riot. Let's go." Davey helped him get his feet moving in the right direction. "I have more 'shine where that came from."

See? Things were looking up already.

* * *

Rebecca lay in embarrassed silence as the ambulance drove them to the hospital. Wonder how good her chances were that no one heard Mitch's little announcement? A glance at the smiling EMT gave her her answer. Damn it.

What was he thinking? They'd carried this secret around for so many years. Nobody was going to understand. Her friends were going to freak out. And what about her mom?

Oh, my God.

"Your heart rate is climbing. Are you in pain?" the paramedic asked, placing two fingers to her wrist and checking her watch.

"No. I really don't need to go to the hospital. You could let me out at the corner. I can walk." She started to sit up but the EMT put a hand to her shoulder, pressing her back down.

"Just let them do their job, honey," Mitch said, humor warming his voice.

Rebecca glared at him. "You're not helping here."

He met her look, unrepentant. Then his gaze roamed her face and the amusement died. His jaw clenched and he nodded toward the injuries. "She going to need stitches?"

The EMT leaned over to check Mitch's forehead. "No, but they'll want to hold her to check for possible concussion."

He hissed and pulled away from her touch. "You too."

"Just take care of Becky, I'm fine."

The paramedic hesitated, then shrugged and sank onto her seat. She picked up a clipboard and started filling in the info. "So, have you two been married long?"

"We're not married," Rebecca answered.

"Five years," Mitch said.

The EMT looked from one to the other of them, eyebrow reaching for her hairline.

Rebecca shot him a shut-up-or-die glare. "We're separated. It's been so long I'd forgotten."

The paramedic eyed them skeptically, then made a note on the clipboard. "Yep. Check for concussions."

Chapter 11

Rebecca was actually glad they had to spend the night in the hospital. The whole episode in the alley had shaken her up more than she'd let anyone know.

Especially Mitch.

He'd resembled an avenging angel bursting out that door and racing to the rescue. Her heart beat a little harder. Thank God they didn't have weapons. As it was, he had a lump the size of a tennis ball on his forehead. By the time the ambulance delivered them to the hospital she'd been worried about his pallor, but none of the nurses who cared for her could fill her in on how he was doing.

By morning she was seriously frazzled. And sore. And she had the headache from hell. Right now nothing sounded better than a hot cup of coffee, some breakfast from Grace's diner, and a long soak in a bubble bath. But first she had to know about Mitch.

She'd just levered herself gingerly up in bed and dropped her legs over the side when the door swung open and he stepped in, charging the room with his presence.

He hesitated when he saw her, a flash of relief turning his lips into a near smile.

"You're up."

He let the door slide closed, sealing them in together, and moved to her side.

"You look like shit." He accompanied the words with a tender kiss to her forehead.

Flustered, she yanked the blanket over her bared legs and used her free hand to try and pat down her bedhead before meeting his gaze. Her eyes widened as she took in the purple coloring that spread upward from his left eye to an impressive sized goose egg.

"Oh, Mitch." Helpless tears formed. She feathered his cheekbone with her fingertips. "I'm so sorry."

He captured her hand and brought it to his lips, releasing her with a gentle squeeze. "You have nothing to be sorry for. I'm just glad I decided to follow you."

Yeah, she was too. Chills broke out when she thought of what could have happened. She shivered.

Mitch glanced around until he spotted a throw blanket folded neatly on a nearby chair. He picked it up and wrapped her shoulders. "You totally rock that hospital green." He grinned.

Grateful for the added warmth, Becky smiled back and struck something of a pose. "You think?"

Mitch's gaze dropped to the gaping V in front. His attention heated her more than any blanket could do. "Oh, yeah."

Uncomfortable, she changed the subject. "Did you get a good look at the guy who hit you?"

Mitch shook his head, wincing a little. "No, but I think I know who it was."

"The same man from the school yesterday." She twisted her hands in her lap. "He recognized me right away."

Mitch swore. "Shit, I knew that guy was bad news. Did you tell the deputies when they came to get our statements last night?"

"It was Jack, and yeah, I told him," she answered. "He said he's working on it."

"Damn rights, since the guy is practically his family." Mitch paced the room.

Rebecca frowned. What was that supposed to mean?

"I think you better explain."

Mitch stopped in front of her and lifted her abused hand in his. "I thought he seemed familiar. It took me a while to figure it out, but then I remembered." He met her confused gaze. "Did you know Jack's first wife, April Montgomery?"

A picture of a beautiful blonde came to mind. She'd been a senior to Rebecca's junior, but still in the same school. They hadn't been friends.

"Yeah, I remember her. She was part of the "*I am*" crowd."

Mitch looked at her quizzically.

"You know. *I am* the prettiest. *I am* a cheerleader." Becky flipped her hair in an imitation of a ditzy chick. "*I am* too good for you."

Mitch smirked. "Yeah, that's the one. She has an older brother. Guess who?"

Rebecca's eyes widened.

Mitch nodded. "That's him. Peter Montgomery, asshole, jackass, and all round dipshit. I guess he hasn't changed."

A young nurse entered the room and strode over wearing squeaky white shoes. "How are we feeling today?" she asked, her eyes going to Mitch for a flirtatious second before she focused on the monitors.

"The doctor should be in soon, then we can remove this…" She lifted Rebecca's hand with the IV attached, "and get you on your way. Sound good?"

Relieved, Becky gave her a friendly smile. "Better than good. No offense, but your coffee doesn't hold a candle to Grits and Grace's."

The nurse laughed. "No offense taken. I go there all the time myself." She glanced at Mitch again, cleared her throat. "Okay, well… I'm just going to check on my other patients. Give me a shout if you need anything." She wrote a quick note on the chart, opened the curtains to let in a stream of light, and left the door open a few inches on her way out.

Rebecca grinned. "She liked you."

Now it was his turn to look uncomfortable. "I never noticed."

Rebecca decided to let him off the hook and returned to their previous subject. "What do you think the connection is between Peter Montgomery and Tommy?"

Mitch shrugged. "Father? Uncle maybe?"

"He didn't really act like a father. More like a guardian or something." Becky thought about how scared Tommy had been. "Whatever the case, I hope Jack can help Tommy. I hate to think of him with that man."

"Jack and I don't always see eye-to-eye, but he's a solid guy. There's no way he'll let a child get injured on his watch." Mitch squeezed her hand. "We'll get this jerk, honey. Don't worry."

Rebecca hoped he was right. There'd been something about those two last night, that even now froze the blood in her veins.

Chapter 12

Tommy glanced to the right, made sure the coast was clear, and waved at his brother to hurry up. Jasper grinned. No doubt this was all a high adventure in his mind. Tommy rolled his hand at him to get a move on. Jasper nodded and stood on tiptoes to reach the shiny red apples in the bin.

Laughter rippled nearby.

Tommy's heart jumped into his throat. He turned and peeked around the next aisle; two teenagers stood in front of a row of magazines giggling over the muscled men on the front cover.

Girls.

A thunderous boom behind made him duck until he realized the noise came from the row where his brother should be. Afraid to look, Tommy peered around the corner and his eyes almost bugged out of his head.

Jasper sat on the floor looking stunned, surrounded by a sea of red. The apple bin lay smashed on its side nearby. The two girls raced past, kicking the fruit aside until they could kneel beside him.

The one with blonde hair leaned over and gave Jasper a quick hug. "Don't cry, little guy. Accidents happen. Mr. Lee is really nice. He won't be mad as long as we clean it all up."

She turned and caught Tommy's eye. "You just going to watch or are you going to help us here?"

He straightened as though he had a broomstick shoved up his spine. Who did she think she was? He'd been taking care of his little brother all the years she was probably playing Barbie.

Embarrassed, he stomped over, picked up an apple, and took a big bite out of it; even though his stomach churned so bad he thought he might puke.

"Quit your cryin', Jasper. It ain't gonna help." He avoided his brother's wide-eyed gaze and wiped the back of his hand across his mouth. "Git up now and give me a hand. I's told ya not to play around them bins."

"But…" Jasper started to protest until he caught his brother's glare and subsided into silence. He climbed sullenly to his feet and began to gather apples into a tumbling pile.

"You don't need to be mean to him. He's just little," the teen scolded.

"And cute," her friend added.

A shuffling step interrupted their happy little group. "What's a happen here?" Mr. Lee, the store owner, came trundling down the aisle, a scowl creasing his already ancient-looking face.

Jasper dropped the fruit he'd been holding and edged behind his brother. Tommy stood taller and attempted to widen his shoulders. He hid the bitten apple behind his back and tried to look innocent. If the old guy called their uncle, they'd be dead for sure.

The blonde girl stood and moved between him and the storeowner, her ponytail swishing back and forth like a horse's tail. "I'm sorry, Mr. Lee. I grabbed an apple from the bottom and it avalanched. I should have known better."

Tommy's mouth dropped open. She'd covered for him.

Mr. Lee tsk, tsked and shuffled by to straighten the bin. He wasn't much taller than Tommy and grunted trying to force it upright. Tommy pushed the apple into his brother's hand and hurried forward, brushing by the flowery smelling girls. Mr. Lee gave him a grateful glance—and didn't that feel great considering he'd just been attempting to steal from the man—and they both put their shoulders to the heavy wooden crate. It crashed down and rocked for a breath-stealing second before settling into place.

"You good boy," Mr. Lee huffed and gave him a toothy grin. He bent with more agility than Tommy expected and tossed him an apple. "You too skinny. Eat."

Tommy caught the fruit and tried to swallow past the hard lump in his throat. He turned away from the teen's soft brown gaze and surreptitiously wiped the moisture from his eyes. He put the apple away in his pocket for later and began gathering the fallen fruit and placing them gently in the righted bin. Jasper joined him first, then the girls.

Blondie met his gaze and smiled. "Hi, I'm Tina."

His face turned hot. He ducked his chin. "I'm Tommy, and this here is Jasper."

"You guys new to town? I haven't seen you around." She dropped an apple in the bin, dusted off her hands, and waited for an answer.

Jasper looked at him nervously and Tommy gave his head a slight shake. "Yeah, we just moved here." He answered, and hoped she'd let it go. Of course she didn't.

"Where are you living? I been here my whole life so I know most areas of town."

"Tommy," Jasper said.

"You're kinda nosy." Tommy tried to change the subject.

Tina giggled. "I've heard that once or twice," she said good-naturedly.

"Tommy," Jasper whined.

"What?" Tommy snapped, turning to glare at his brother. Jasper pointed, and Tommy's stomach plunged down to his toes. A man built like the Hulk stood beside Mr. Lee, and he had a gun.

Chapter 13

When Jack Garrett entered the Pine Bluff Corner Store on his way home from work, the last thing he expected to see was his daughter in the midst of what seemed to have been an apple free-for-all.

Just once couldn't his day be normal?

Sighing, he stepped forward to offer a hand and that's when he noticed the two young boys. The youngest was chomping his way through an apple twice the size of his grubby hands, reddish-blond hair sticking straight up in the back. The other kid looked to be a couple years older with bedraggled clothes and dirty brown hair. He was grinning at something Tina must have said as he carefully set a couple pieces of fruit in the bin.

She smiled back, and Jack's stomach dropped into his shoes. They wore the exact same expression. These were April's kids. Mitch was right.

The older one turned just then and got an eyeball full of Jack and his holstered weapon. The shock would have been comical except for the fact he could relate. He was feeling a little—okay, a lot—flummoxed himself.

Tina noticed him and ran forward. "Hi, Daddy."

At the same second, Jack saw the kid perform a set of hand signals worthy of a pro baseball catcher. The younger one nodded and disappeared around the bottom of the aisle.

Shit.

"Hey, hold up there," he called, and took a step, only to almost land on his ass when an apple rolled under his foot.

The older kid, seeing his chance, turned and dived around the end of the bin.

"Stop," Jack yelled, arms flailing as he tried to regain his balance.

"Daddy," Tina cried, screeching to a halt looking dazed and bewildered.

Join the crowd.

Mr. Lee was chanting some kind of Chinese mumbo-jumbo, his frail arms crossed and head bobbing up and down.

"Dad, wait."

Jack grabbed his cell and dialed the station. "Not now, Tina. I'll explain later."

Much later, if he had his way.

"You read my mind," Laurel purred. "Grab some strawberries and whipped cream on your way home, honey. I have plans."

Oh, yeah.

"Do you always answer the phone that way?" He smiled, momentarily lulled by the image she'd placed in his head. "What if it wasn't your husband?"

"Oops. Jack, is that you?" she teased.

He laughed outright, then got reluctantly back to business. "We'll talk about your insubordination later. Right now I need you to send a car to the Corner Store, stat."

"Oh, Jack. Are you okay?"

"I'm fine, just walked in on a bit of a disturbance." He picked his way more carefully through the little red landmines waiting to trip him up. "I need someone to help take statements, that's all."

He'd have to tell Laurel and his daughter the whole story at some point, but he wasn't sure how to go about it. *Hey, Tina, guess what? You have a couple of step-brothers.*

Color him excited.

He caught a glimpse of blond hair near the paper product aisle and snuck down the cat food row to catch him on the other end. Except he must have made more noise than he thought, because when he rounded the corner he was met by a hailstorm of TP.

What the…?

A roll bounced off the top of his head and tumbled down his shoulder, leaving a trail of white tissue in its wake. His eyes narrowed. This was getting out of hand. The culprits stood about five feet away doing an impressive job of holding him back— for the moment.

He raised his arm as a shield and forged ahead, refusing to be outdone by a snot-nosed brat. And that's where he made his mistake.

* * *

Mitch opened the door to the grocery store and couldn't believe his eyes. It looked as though a bomb had gone off. Apples lay all over the produce section and Mr. Lee rocked back and forth yelling something in Mandarin that made no sense at all. Something about guns and kids and toilet paper?

It was like a scene from *The Twilight Zone*.

He glanced out the glass door and made sure Becky was still in the truck. Last thing he needed was her getting hurt again. Her gaze was on something in her lap—cell phone probably—so he headed straight for Tina who was wringing her hands and staring toward the back of the store.

"What's going on?" he asked, nodding toward the mess.

She turned a distraught puppy-dog gaze on him that about melted his heart.

"My dad thinks two boys did this deliberately, but they didn't." Her tone said her dad was an idiot sometimes. Mitch couldn't argue the point. "He chased after them, even though I tried to tell him."

He knew he should have stopped at the supermarket instead. *Dammit.*

"I'll see if he needs a hand. You take care of Mr. Lee, okay? And if you see Miss Sorenson come in, keep her here." He waited for her to nod her understanding then hurried in the direction of war-whoops and crashing shelves, not sure what to expect.

It sure wasn't finding Jack on his ass, a shelving unit across his legs, and unraveled toilet paper decorating his head and shoulders.

Mitch skidded to a halt, a slow grin lighting his lips. Jack looked up from where he'd been trying to extricate himself from the mess and swore.

"Hey, big guy. Life got you down in the dumps? Just try a roll of this, it's guaranteed to cushion your fall."

"Oh, you're a barrel of laughs," Jack growled. "Help me up."

Mitch pulled his phone out and snapped a couple quick shots first.

Never know when they might come in handy.

Chapter 14

Rebecca finished checking her newsfeeds, moved on to texting her mom that she was okay, and no she didn't need to cancel her trip, and still, Mitch hadn't returned from the store. What was he doing, buying the place out? She wanted to get home and have a long, hot shower in the worst way.

Lowering the visor, she inspected the bruising on her face, relieved that most of the swelling had gone down and she didn't resemble the train wreck her body felt like it had been through. Funny how a few chance events can change the course of one's life. If anyone had told her a few days ago that she would be sitting in her ex-husband's vehicle anxiously waiting for his return, she'd have asked them if they'd taken a recent trip into la-la land.

Where is he?

She opened the door and slid out of the cab. What is it with guys and big trucks? She yanked her skirt down where it had ridden up, grimacing at the picture she must make. Flyaway hair, a beat-up face, and last night's party clothes—now dirty and wrinkled—not exactly haute couture.

Shrugging away her vanity, Rebecca marched toward the store, but halted when she heard pounding feet coming from the far side of the building. A tow-headed boy appeared, running like the hounds of hell were after him, but his attention was on something behind him and he didn't see the low parking barricade he was about to run into.

"Look out," Becky called.

He glanced back, startled, but it was too late. His foot caught the meridian and he went flying over the top, landing in a heap on the other side.

Rebecca gasped, picked up her long skirts, and ran.

Another boy appeared and zipped across the lot to the fallen kid. When she arrived and crouched to help the crying child, Tommy's familiar fear-filled brown eyes greeted her. His gaze widened on her bruised face, then he eyed the little guy's rapidly swelling ankle and tears formed.

"Please, Miss, that's my brother. You gotta help him," Tommy begged, rocking back and forth on his heels. "Don't cry, Jasper. It's gonna be okay, just please don't cry."

Rebecca smiled reassuringly, though she could see that it was most likely a break. Poor guy. Her heart squeezed in sympathy. "I'm afraid he might have a broken leg. Let me see your hands, buddy. Did they get hurt too?" She lifted the hand he was cradling in his lap and cringed. The skin was scraped, with little pebbles poking out of the lacerations. It looked very painful.

Tommy blanched and then the tears did fall. "I'm sorry, Jasper. I should've left you at home."

Jasper used the least damaged hand to pat his brother's shoulder. "It's not your fault, Tommy. I shoulda been looking where I was runnin'. I messed up, didn't I? *He's* gonna be mad."

An instant vision of the previous night's assault pebbled Becky's skin with revulsion. If these kids had to put up with even an ounce of what she had...

"Who is he talking about?" She leaned forward and grasped Tommy's knee. "I want to help you and your brother, but you have to trust me. Can you do that?" Shivers racked his narrow frame and Becky ached to take them both in her arms, but she respected their reserve. How could anyone treat little children the way she suspected these two had been handled? It made her blood boil to think of it.

Tommy eyed her for a long moment then seemed to come to a decision, his shoulders bowing from untold months of stress. "He's our uncle. Momma... she ain't alive no more, and the child welfare people made us come live here with *him*."

He looked up and hatred shone from eyes that held a wealth of horrible experiences. It broke her heart.

"Oh, honey." She gave in and tugged him close, even though it was like holding a steel pole. "Don't you worry, you aren't ever going to have to stay there again. I promise." She gave Jasper a watery smile and set Tommy back. "Okay, let's get your brother some help, shall we?"

Just then Jack and Mitch came tumbling out the back door and Tommy scrambled to his feet, his eyes desperate.

"Tommy, don't leave me," Jasper cried, clearly scared.

Tommy mouth turned down. "As if I would," he said, squaring his shoulders and stepping in front of his brother. "You better leave us alone," he shouted at the men.

Rebecca saw when Mitch caught sight of her sitting on the ground. He shook his head, ignored the warning, and strode to her side, dropping down on his haunches. "You couldn't just wait in the truck, huh?" he teased, and ran a light finger down her cheek.

Becky's skin zinged, the sparks zapping between them.

Mitch's gaze zeroed in on her lips and darkened. "You and me—later. I'm tired of waiting. It's time we settled our past so we can move forward with our lives." He leaned in and gave her a quick, hard kiss, their breath co-mingling and tasting of the coffee he'd stopped and bought for her.

Rebecca sighed and gave herself up to the moment, though in the back of her mind his words nipped and stung, warning her that it was going to hurt when he left. How did this happen? When did Mitch Taylor become necessary to her happiness?

God. She was in love with him.

Her mouth slackened. Mitch sat back and looked at her quizzically for a moment, then he turned away to help young Jasper, and she tried to pay attention, she really did. But, all the time he was asking Tommy what happened, and running gentle fingers over the injury, and she was smiling and murmuring reassurance, her heart was breaking into a million tiny pieces.

Chapter 15

When had his life become so difficult? Mitch kept sneaking glances at Becky while trying to determine the kid's injuries and not get stabbed in the back by the older boy. And what the hell was Jack doing? He stood a few feet away with a cell phone plastered to his ear and brows drawn in a forbidding line. No wonder the kid had freaked out. Jack didn't have the friendliest looking mug at the best of times, never mind when he figured someone was messing with his precious town.

The boy cried out when he touched a particularly tender area and his cornflower blue eyes filled with tears. Becky tut-tutted and sent Mitch a reproachful look before sliding her hand over the kid's.

"Shh, he didn't mean to, honey. The sheriff is probably calling for help right now. We'll get you fixed up and on your feet again in no time."

Tommy shook his head. "He cain't go to no doctor. We's got no money." He made rabbit ears of his pockets to prove his point.

Mitch smiled to ease the boy's mind. "Don't worry about the bill. The sheriff will handle it," he said, noticing Jack had moved closer to the group.

Jack let out a loud harrumph, and ignored him to look at Rebecca, his face softening with empathy. "How are you doing? Sorry we didn't make it up to the hospital, Laurel wasn't feeling too good this morning. She was some upset when she heard about what happened." He slid a glance at the kids. "You find out anything?"

She gave a slight nod. "I'll explain later. Is help on the way? He's being so brave." The boy's attention wavered between them.

Jack shifted and Tommy cringed, backing up a step and damn near landing on his brother. Mitch reached out and steadied him before letting go. He shot Jack a warning glance. These kids were gun-shy. For some reason they had decided to trust Becky, and by default himself, but that's as far as they were willing to go. Going by last night's little misadventure, he couldn't blame them. It pissed him off all over again thinking about those assholes hurting either child.

Jack looked hurt, concern turning his face into a grim mask. He loved his daughter so much; everyone knew it, so Mitch had no doubt that it was painful the children were leery with him. It was kind of odd that they were okay around him, he'd never had anything to do with kids. Not many around his line of work. Which led him back to Rebecca. Her life revolved around children; secretary at the elementary school, her friends and their kids. He had no place in that life.

She deserved someone who could give her the moon, all he could offer was a slice of cheese. The best thing he could do was sign the divorce papers and step back, let her go. Even if it Broke. His. Goddamn. Heart.

And it would. Mitch had no doubt of that now. He'd managed to stuff his feelings down deep inside, but the truth was, from the moment he'd laid eyes on her all those years ago, he'd known. She was The One.

He'd never really moved on since. There'd been a few women—he was a normal, healthy male—but none that connected on the same wavelength as Rebecca. She was his missing piece.

And because of that he wanted what was best for her, which didn't include a dumb tradesman like himself.

"Here comes the ambulance now," Jack said, and waved them over when they turned into the lot.

"I'm scared," Jasper whispered, his face shades lighter than the pavement he was laying on.

Tommy knelt on the ground and gave his brother a fierce hug. "It's going to be okay, Jas. Just think, we get to ride in an ambulance."

Mitch swallowed around the lump in his throat. Tommy wasn't much older than his kid brother, but had taken on the role of provider just the same. Mitch planned on making it his business that useless piece of skin they had the misfortune to call an uncle never came near any of them again. He glanced at Jack and caught the exact same emotion shining out of his eyes. Their gazes met in a rare moment of solidarity and the lump grew to mammoth proportions.

"Can I ride with you guys?" Rebecca asked the boys. "I love ambulances. Maybe they'll even flash their lights for us."

Mitch gave her an incredulous look, though he shouldn't be surprised. Of course she'd set aside her own comfort if it meant helping kids. His heart pinched. He loved her so damn much it hurt.

He cleared his throat and stood out of the way as the EMTs took over. Jasper kept a death grip on Becky's hand the entire time they splinted his leg then loaded him onto a stretcher and wheeled it to the back of the vehicle, Tommy dogging their heels.

She glanced back, and something like regret chased shadows across her face, then they were gone with a squeal of tires and the requested blare of sirens.

The parking lot seemed dull and dismal after she left. The thought of losing the right to call her his wife ripped a hole in his gut.

"You comin'?" Jack asked.

Mitch shrugged off the black mood and nodded. "Where we headed?"

"That was Sid, my deputy. He has a lead on the location of our perp. Thought I'd take a drive and check it out."

Anticipation zipped through Mitch's veins. Damn right he wanted to catch up to the creeps. "I'm in, let's go." He started toward the front of the store where his truck was parked.

"Hey, Mitch," Jack called.

Mitch turned, impatient to get a move on and maybe release some of his inner tension on a face or two.

"Look, about before," Jack said. "You know, with April." He glanced down, then looked Mitch square in the eye. "It's been a long time, man. Let's put it behind us, agreed?"

Mitch hesitated. If he kept his mouth shut, the whole episode could be put to rest. Forgiven if not forgotten. It wasn't enough though. He needed to clean the slate. Until April pulled her little stunt, the men had been as close as those two brothers they'd just placed in the ambulance. It was long past due that they cleared the air between them.

"April Montgomery was a beautiful woman," he started, then hurried on when Jack stiffened. "But, she was *your* woman, Jack. I know you figured we had something going on, and hell, I wouldn't put it past her to foster that impression, but I swear to you we didn't."

He kicked a rock and listened to it ping off the garbage dumpster. "Listen, I know you loved her and all, but there was something seriously wrong with her. She thrived on making you jealous. You have to see that, right?"

Jack stood as though frozen in time, and maybe he was. April had single-handedly destroyed not only their friendship, but also two promising careers. Not to mention abandoning a child. She would never rate for any mother of the year awards, that's for damn sure.

"So all this time, while I've been wondering if Tina was mine," Jack growled, but before he could finish what he was going to say they heard a gasping cry from behind.

Tina stood near the open back door, hands over her mouth and tears streaming down her white face.

"Tina," Jack croaked.

She turned and blindly stumbled toward the door.

"Honey, wait."

But, it was too late. She was gone.

Chapter 16

Pete woke up to the strident ringing of the telephone. His face was plastered to the floor and it felt like a ten-piece band was rehearsing in his skull. *Ugh.* His mouth tasted like somethin' crawled up and died in there. It took him two tries to lift his head and focus bleary eyes on Davey passed out at the kitchen table, a half-full glass of rotgut still in his hand.

Sunlight seeped through the gaps around the front door and fought with the dirty windowpanes to stream into the room and push away the gloom. He'd told that fricken kid to keep them curtains closed, dammit. A surge of bile rose and he forced himself to his feet, barely managing to bounce off the hall walls and make it to the can in time. Grimacing, he bent under the tap and rinsed with lukewarm water, then sluiced it over his head, hoping for some clarity. The red-rimmed gaze that met him in the veined mirror wasn't encouraging.

It was those kids' fucking fault. If they hadn't stressed him out... He ignored the fact that he'd been drinking like this long before they came on the scene. What the hell did he know about kids? Why his sister named him their guardian, he'd never know. The only good thing to come out of this mess was the money. April had done good for herself—a fuck of a lot better than she had in this shithole. If not for the accident, she'd promised to take care of him, maybe even bring him out there to L.A. to live with her and that high-falutin' dentist husband of hers. Now that dream was gone.

But not the money.

As the only living relative, he'd been appointed trustee of the kids' inheritance. It wasn't his fault it took a lot to live these days. Speaking of which... where the hell were they? Usually the youngest one was driving him up the bend by now with the noise he made. He'd had to lay down the law a couple of times already. Pete rubbed his bristly jaw and thought about the welts he'd caused on the kid's back. Remorse rode the waves of discomfort rolling in his gut. He hadn't meant to, he weren't no molester. It's just the noise about drove him nuts. The kid would learn. He'd better. They were a team now; they had to figure out how to get along.

He staggered back down the hall, his legs still unsteady, and gave Davey a shove, frowning when the hooch sloshed over the rim of the glass. He snagged it as the other man moaned and groaned the stupor away.

"What the hell, man?" Davey whispered, his voice hoarse.

"Get up. You gotta help me find those brats."

Davey wiped the drool off his face. "Fuck, man, they're probably out in the yard. What's the big deal?"

Pete sucked back the booze, closing his eyes to relish the shiver that worked its way down his spine. "The deal is that I said it's time to git up." He kicked the leg of the chair. "Now move."

Davey shot him a death wish glare laced with uncertainty—guy was smarter than he looked—and lurched to his feet. "Whatever, man."

Satisfied, Pete threw open the door and growled as the light pierced his eyeballs. Shit, that hurt.

When he thought he could move without his head exploding, he pitched down the stairs and into the dirt yard. Nothing stirred. What the hell? He waved Davey around the other side and then went left himself, heading for the kid's homemade sandpit. Nothing but a damn Tonka toy. He picked it up and hurled it into the trees just as Davey showed up shaking his head.

He was gonna kill those little fucks.

Chapter 17

By the time Rebecca arrived home from the hospital she was tired and sore, but relieved Jasper's ankle had turned out to be a bad sprain, instead of broken. The kids were in her living room now, eating grilled cheese sandwiches with giant glasses of milk, and watching superhero cartoons while she… she was finally having that hot bath she'd been dreaming about.

And *boy*, did it feel good.

She leaned back in the clawfoot tub and closed her eyes, relaxing for the first time in days. Aching muscles sang *hallelujah* as the warm water and soapy bubbles did their job. Her lips twitched at the muted sound of the television and childish laughter coming from the other room. Ever since her mom bought a condo in the new senior's subdivision, Rebecca had been alone in the house. She thought she liked it that way, but this was… nice.

Jack had cleared it with Social Services so the boys could come home with her. Eventually more permanent arrangements would have to be made, but for now at least, they were safe. Unfortunately, cases like this happened all too often. Working within the school system, teachers and staff were often the first line of defense for children like Tommy and Jasper. It wasn't right, and it wasn't fair, it just was.

She ran a finger along the scar under her ear and remembered a time when she'd been grateful for a teacher's intervention. If it were up to her no child would ever go hungry or be afraid in their own home. Tommy was too young to have to take on the responsibility of his brother. He'd done the best that he could.

Mr. Lee called the hospital while they were there and reassured her there would be no charges, but he wanted Tommy to come and help at the store to make up for what he'd done. Tommy had been stunned when she'd relayed the message. Obviously, he was used to a more substantial punishment. Not any more. Not if she had any say in the matter.

Rebecca woke sometime later, chilled. She sat up, sloshing water against the sides of the deep bathtub. Her hair had slipped its topknot and now lay suctioned against her goose-pimply arms and chest. Shoot, some caregiver she was.

The television still blared, though she couldn't hear the kids any more. Maybe they'd followed her example and fallen asleep on the sofa.

She looked down and grimaced. Half-dry soap bubbles covered her upper body. She hurried to sluice off, shivering as the cool washcloth passed over her skin. Catching the chain with her toe, she pulled the plug, then stood and stepped out onto a plush white bathmat. Reaching over to the hook on the door, she grabbed the navy blue bathtowel and hurried to dry herself before slipping into her cotton candy pink robe and snuggling into its enveloping warmth.

The bang of the back door and a child's cry halted the combing of her damp hair. She opened the door and padded in bare feet down the carpeted corridor. She peeked into the living room on the right. *Spiderman* was climbing the outside of a building on the TV, but no one was watching him. The kids' plates sat empty where she'd left them on the coffee table, the milk half drunk.

Concerned, she turned and hurried the rest of the way down the hall to the kitchen. Maybe they were still hungry and had gone looking for food. She hoped Tommy had the sense not to use the stove to make more grilled sandwiches.

Rounding the corner, she shrieked. Two men sat at her kitchen table wolfing down what seemed like the entire contents of her fridge. Tommy and Jasper were on the floor near the back door. Tommy had an arm around his brother's shoulders. Tears had left tracks down both boys' cheeks. All four looked up when she entered the room and her hands fluttered up to the edges of her robe.

"Well, if it ain't the teach." The heavier-set man—Tommy's uncle, she was sure—plucked at his yellowed teeth with a toothpick. "We were wondering where you were. Not very nice leavin' kids by themselves. No tellin' how much trouble they'll git into."

"I told ya I'd go git her," the other guy said. His smarmy gaze made her feel as though she were naked even though the robe covered her from head to toe.

"What are you doing here?" she demanded. The unwashed stench of sweat and alcohol permeating the room from their bodies was awful. It also warned her as nothing else could that these were desperate men with nothing left to lose.

"They…" Tommy started to rise, but a warning glare from his uncle had him sinking down again, sullen and angry.

Rebecca gave her head the slightest shake. *Please don't do anything stupid.*

"Shut your trap, boy. You're lucky I didn't beat your ass for taking off like that." He took a long chug of milk—right out of the carton—then focused on Becky. "What did you do to my littlest boy, Teach? That how you treat kids in that fancy school of yours? Imagine my surprise to hear a message from the hospital saying you'd been givin' permission to bring them home—prior to an investigation."

Rebecca gasped. He was trying to blame Jasper's accident on her? "If you had food for them to eat, they wouldn't have been trying to steal some."

The moment the words left her lips she knew it was the wrong thing to say. Pete turned his attention to Tommy who cowered into the corner. Jasper started sobbing and covered his head with his arm, bandaged leg sticking vulnerably at an angle from his body.

Pete stood, the chair scraping on the ceramic tiles. His fist clenched around the carton, and milk gushed over the top of his hand. Swearing, he threw the container and it splattered on the wall above the boys' heads.

Incensed, Becky screeched and ran toward him, fists raised to pound some sense into the idiot. She never got the chance.

The other man came at her from the side and knocked her to her knees, his weight driving her facedown onto the floor. Panicking, she bucked and twisted, desperate to get him off her, but he only laughed and dug his bony hand into the center of her back to hold her still.

"I knew you'd like it rough," he said. "You and I have unfinished business, Teach.

"You let her go," Tommy cried.

Becky turned her head in time to see him jump to his feet and try to lunge across the distance between them, but his uncle grabbed him by the back of his shirt and stopped his momentum.

He gave the kid a little shake and sent him stumbling back to his brother. "You heard the kid, Davey. We didn't come here for none of that crap. She'll just get us into a world of trouble. Let's go, man. We got what we came for."

Davey swore and Becky could feel him shake his head above her. "Nah, you want to wuss out, go ahead. I'm good right where I am." He rubbed his hand along her hip and helpless tears sprang into Becky's eyes.

There was a moment's silence when all she could hear was her terrified breaths and Jasper's sobs, then Pete gave a harsh laugh and said, "Whatever, man. It's your funeral."

Black work boots with undone laces shuffled into her line of vision. "You sure, Dave? This is a felony. You could do jail time, man."

Davey shifted, his weight squeezing all the air out of her lungs. Or maybe that was the fear.

"They gotta catch me first," Davey answered, his hand petting her hair like she was some sort of dog. "Don't worry, I'll catch up with you later and tell ya all about it over a drink or two." Rough laughter erupted, then the boots moved away and her heart intensified its already staccato beat.

She filled her head with visions of Mitch. The prospect of his warm smile and strong arms wrapping her in safety and love. The taste of his kisses and the goal of a future together would be her reason for succeeding. That, and the fact that she refused to go down without a fight. How was she going to get out of this? He was too strong to overpower. She needed a weapon…

Her comb.

It was in the pocket of her robe. If she could just get her hands on it, she might have a slim chance. Possibly, her only chance

Chapter 18

Mitch glanced over at Jack's clenched hands on the steering wheel and the grim line of his jaw. He wished there was something he could say. If only Tina had waited for an explanation.

"Jack, I'm sorry I brought all that shit up. This should never have happened." He turned his gaze to the front, hoping against hope to catch a glimpse of the girl. "We'll find her, she couldn't have gone far."

"And then what?" Jack growled. "I tell her her mother was a whore who'd split her legs for anyone willing to pay?" He slapped the steering wheel. "I can't believe I said that back there. Of course she's my daughter, blood or no blood. I don't really give a fuck. She's been mine since the day she was born."

He rolled down the windows and the smell of fresh-cut grass swept into the car. There was nothing except the sound of the Mustang's powerful engine for a couple of blocks, then Jack sighed. "I never blamed you, you know." He glanced at Mitch. "I knew what April was like, but she had her hooks in me good. And then, when things fell apart, I needed a scapegoat. After all, it couldn't be my fault we failed, right?" His laugh was cynical.

Mitch frowned. That damn woman had a lot to answer for.

They turned the corner and motored down Becky's street. He glanced out the window to see if she'd made it home from the hospital yet.

"Stop." His breath backed up his throat. "There, in the alley. See that?" He pointed to the half-hidden nose of a dusty red truck. "I think that's Pete Montgomery's pick-up. What the hell is he doing here?"

Jack drove past and parked a couple of houses down the street. He threw his arm over the seat and gazed through the back window while Mitch stared out his side mirror, his hand on the door handle.

"Hold on," Jack warned. "We don't want to go rushing in there and make things worse. You stay here, and I'll go have a look around. Call for back-up."

Mitch opened his door and was out of the car before Jack could stop him. "Like that's gonna happen."

Jack climbed out and glared over the roof. "Fine. Then we do this my way. We don't want to give away our position until we know what we're dealing with, so you go around the far side and check the windows—carefully—and I'll do this side. We'll meet in the back yard. Good?"

Mitch hesitated. His instincts were shouting at him to get to his woman, but he could see the validity of Jack's plan. They had to make sure she was safe first. But God wouldn't be able to help the son-of-a-bitch if he'd done anything to hurt her.

Mitch reluctantly nodded, waiting impatiently while Jack called it in, and then they were on the move.

The first two sets of windows had drawn curtains, ramping his anxiety levels into the stratosphere. The next one was her office, dark except for the glowing computer. He had to negotiate his way through a rhododendron to get to the next window, the living room. The blinds were pulled but there was just enough room for him to see it too was empty, though the television was on, so someone was definitely home.

Where was she? Maybe he was wrong and that was just a neighbor's truck, but something told him it was more. His heart throbbed in time with the words running through his head, *hurry, hurry before it's too late*.

He pushed his way out of the bushes, careful to make as little noise as possible, and rounded the corner into the back yard. Jack stood, hands raised in front of him, in the middle of the yard. What the…?

Mitch faded into the old house's shadow and tried to get a handle on what was happening. At first he couldn't see anything, but then the kid, Tommy, stumbled into view with an arm around his brother's waist, acting as a crutch. They started a hobbling run, but froze when someone yelled at them from the house.

"You kids stop right there or you won't be sitting down for a week once we get home. You're lucky I haven't punished you already."

Mitch swore long and fluidly under his breath. He'd been right, Tommy's uncle was here. Where was Rebecca?

"Let them go, Montgomery. My men are on the way." Jack turned his hands over in a pleading gesture. "Please, Pete. She doesn't have anything to do with this." The raw emotion pouring from his friend's voice told Mitch what was going on before he even saw the blonde head forced back against Montgomery's shoulder, his hand wrapped around her neck.

Fuck. What was Tina doing in the middle of this mess?

"Does *she* know we're kin, Jack?" Pete's laugh was harsh. He jerked his head to the left and the boys slowly made their way toward the pick-up. "Yeah, I thought not. Stay back and I'll let 'er go. Get in my way and you won't like the consequences."

"Daddy…" Tina's cry was agonizing.

Mitch's hands clenched. He edged along the wall, waiting for an opportunity to jump the bastard without hurting Jack's daughter. A fleeting glance showed Jack doing the same, his face a grim mask. Suddenly, Tina tripped and gave Jack the time he needed to sack Pete in an impressive interception worthy of *Heisman* consideration.

The two rolled on the ground until Jack got the upper-hand with a clip to the jaw that put the other man down. He pulled his cuffs and yelled, "Go."

He didn't need to be told twice.

With a quick check to make sure Tina was okay, Mitch jumped the porch stairs and threw himself against the half-closed door. It slammed back on its hinges and revealed a scene right out of his worst nightmares.

Becky lay sprawled out on the kitchen floor, her housecoat up around her thighs as she fought to unseat the man on her back. He had her hair wrapped around his fist, and when Mitch entered the room, he gave it a vicious twist, causing her to cry out in pain.

He looked up and grinned, his blackened teeth turning Mitch's stomach. "Seems like we been here before, don't it?" The smile faded and something dark and ugly took its place. "You want to see her live, I suggest you back your ass right out that there door. It'd be a shame if her neck *accidently* snapped."

Mitch froze, except for the muscle in his cheek jumping uncontrollably.

"I'm going to rip you apart." He gritted through clenched teeth. It was an oath. One he intended to keep.

Rebecca tried to meet his gaze and the fucker slammed her head onto the floor.

Mitch exploded.

He copied Jack's move, albeit not as gracefully, and plowed headfirst into the asshole's chest. The momentum sent them flying backward against the far wall. Mitch shook his head, dazed. The other guy lifted his knee and nailed him in the sack.

Fuuuck, that hurt.

Stunned, Mitch rolled to the side, his body going fetal as sparks jumped behind his eyelids. A booted foot kicked him in the ribs repeatedly until he managed to lash out and knock the prick off his feet.

He inhaled a pained breath, turned to finish the fight… and sat up in shock.

Rebecca perched on the guy's chest, a Valkyrie come to life. She'd pounced and had a rat tail comb poised near his jugular. Her hair resembled a porcupine having a bad day, and her cheeks were flushed as pink as her god-awful robe. She wore the biggest victory smirk he'd ever witnessed. He'd never seen anything more beautiful.

"I guess you got your man," he said, his voice hoarse.

She met his gaze and the love shining out of those impossibly blue eyes made him feel like he'd taken a trip to heaven.

"Yes," she said. "I think I have."

Chapter 19

Rebecca sipped her coffee and smiled absently to Susan's chatter, until she mentioned how lucky she was, and how her mom would have a conniption fit if she knew what happened.

"Don't call her, Susan, please." She met the worried gaze of her mom's best friend and reached out to grasp her hand. "I'm fine. Mom's having the holiday she always dreamed of. I don't want her to cut it short because of me."

Susan set the coffee pot on the café tabletop and leaned over to give her a swift hug. "Okay, sugar, but don't you go scarin' me like that again, you hear?"

Becky laughed. "Not if I can help it."

She was just grateful Jack's deputies had arrived in time to assist in the arrest of Tommy and Jasper's uncle and his asshole friend.

Someone hollered down the way, and Susan grimaced "Hold yer horses, Phil, I'm coming."

She picked up the pot, winked at Becky, and was gone, a bright ray of sunshine with her bleached blonde hair highlighted by a neon green streak running down the side, and her crazy assortment of jewelry. Today she wore Elvis Presley earrings from his Vegas show, the cape and belt glowing with rhinestones.

The bell tinkling above the door drew Rebecca's attention. Her heart stuttered as Mitch walked in, his arms loaded with the biggest bouquet of daisies she'd ever seen. The room grew quiet as he drew closer, but Becky barely noticed. This man was her husband. Why did it take a near catastrophe for her to realize how very important he was to her existence?

"Hi," he murmured, handing the flowers over.

She buried her face in them until she could get her thoughts together. She'd mentioned how much she loved daisies way back when they'd spent that evening in Las Vegas getting to know each other.

And he'd remembered.

His big body slid onto the bench beside her and his arm went around her waist before she felt able to lift her head without bursting into tears.

"They're beautiful," she whispered, her gaze on his dear face.

"So… are you ready to give us a shot now?" he asked, his expression vulnerable.

Happy beyond words, she nodded and threw herself into the haven of his arms.

"Yay, the teacher said yes," Tommy cried.

Becky looked up, surprised, and noticed their friends surrounding the table. From a grinning Jack, his arms wrapped around Laurel and Tina, who hadn't been harmed in the incident, thank God. Becky would never forget her fear when Pete opened the kitchen door and Tina was there. She'd fought with her dad and come searching for the boys after finding out the shocking news that they were her stepbrothers. It would take some time but Jack was a great father—he'd work it out.

Next, Becky's teary gaze moved on to Ty and Katy, Katy's baby bump pronounced in the summer dress she was wearing.

Mitch's buddy, Jared, stood off to the side, a knowing smirk on his lips, his wife-to-be, Annie, tucked in front of him. Grace stepped forward, a gorgeous wedding cake in her hands.

Becky turned a bemused gaze on Mitch. "They know?"

He turned faintly red. "I wasn't going to give you a chance to run away this time."

Rebecca didn't know what to say.

"Miss Sorenson." Tommy stood at her elbow, his hand held out to show a fragile gold chain.

Tears leaked down Becky's face as she reached out and lifted the locket from his palm.

"You found it."

She ran a finger over the filigree workmanship and gave Tommy a watery smile before glancing shyly at Mitch. "Do you remember this?"

A look of wonder turned his eyes almost the same shade of gold. "I bought you that for a wedding gift. You kept it," he said with a quiet satisfaction.

"Of course," she answered. "When the man you love buys you a gift, you hang on to it."

Mitch leaned down and placed his lips to hers.

"Forever," he said.

"Forever," she agreed.

Afterword

Reviews are the lifeblood of any successful author. Without you, we can't be heard.

If you enjoy the story, please consider sharing on your favorite social media sites, as well as GoodReads and from wherever you've bought the book.

Thank you,

Jacquie Biggar

Jacqbiggar.com

About the Author

Jacquie writes Romantic Suspense with tough, alpha males who know what they want, until they're gob-smacked by heroines who are strong, contemporary women willing to show them that what they really need is love.

She has been blessed with a long, happy marriage and enjoys writing romance novels that end with happy-ever-afters.

Jacquie lives in paradise along the west coast of Canada with her family and loves reading, writing, and flower gardening. She swears she can't function without coffee, preferably at the beach with her sweetheart. :)

Follow Jacquie's website below - if you check out her giveaways page you'll find tons of great prizes every month!

Newsletter- http://eepurl.com/2MFvX

Also by Jacquie Biggar

Tidal Falls- #1 Wounded Hearts

The Rebel's Redemption- #2 Wounded Hearts

Twilight's Encore- #3 Wounded Hearts

The Sheriff Meets His Match- #4 Wounded Hearts

Summer Lovin'- #5 Wounded Hearts

The Guardian- #1 Mended Souls

Preview The Guardian

by Jacquie Biggar

Chapter One

If Lucas Carmichael had known he was going to wake up dead, he might have kept sleeping.

There was some sort of a thin sheet covering him from head to toe, but it didn't do anything to stop his body from shaking or his heels from vibrating on the table beneath him. His chest pumped like a set of bellows on steroids. He blinked repeatedly to get his bearings, but still couldn't see a fricking thing.

What the hell was going on?

A white-hot pain hit him between the brows.

Ow.

He rubbed his forehead. Except—his palms were still on the cold metal of the table. He could feel them there. So, whose…?

Adrenaline spiked, shooting adrenaline though his system.

Terrified, he shoved off the choking hold of the sheet and threw himself to the floor, crouching for a moment to get his bearings, every muscle tensed. Reaction set in and perspiration broke over his naked body, rattling his teeth. A high-pitched whistle rang in his ears, and his heart pounded harder than his old base speaker beating out a Black Sabbath tune.

He squinted against the lights, blindingly bright after the darkness of the sheet. A man and a woman stood a few feet away behind another table with a blanket shrouded figure. Weird. They hadn't even glanced up when he performed his gymnastics. Something strange was going on here.

"It's too bad. She had her whole life in front of her," the woman said as she took some sort of vise and lodged it in the poor sucker's chest. "I heard they were headed from a party when it happened."

The other guy in a white jacket shook his head. "These guys never learn. They think just because they're the newest hot item and have more money than God, nothing's ever going to happen to them."

He reached into the cavity and carefully removed what looked like the heart and placed it in a pan resting on the corpse's legs. "At least she'll make a good research candidate."

Holy shit.

He was in a freaking morgue. How the hell did that happen? Last thing he remembered was cruisin' down the highway in his new 911 Porsche with the music blaring so loud he could barely hear himself think. His best friend, Scott, with his younger sister, Natalya, on his lap in the passenger seat, had just glanced over her blond head and smiled the quirky grin that had won him instant box office success.

Lucas remembered thinking they were so freaking lucky—to come from where they had, to where they were now? A miracle.

He'd laughed and turned back to the curves of the road, but his vision went wonky for a second. When it straightened out his eyes had widened in shock. The sharp tang of copper flooded his mouth.

The windshield was filled with the terrified faces of the family in a van hurtling straight toward them. Shit, he must have swerved over the center line.

They were going to crash.

Time simultaneously slowed to a crawl, and jumped to warp speed. The man was frantically trying to turn the wheel and avoid the collision, while the woman's horrified face stared accusingly at him out the window before she turned to the back seat in a vain effort to protect her babies. Those images would haunt him for the rest of his days.

A litany of prayers Lucas hadn't uttered since he'd been a young child rattled off his lips while Scott's "What the fuck?" vibrated with fear. He felt more than saw his friend bracing for impact, his arms tightening around Nat as he buried her face in his shoulder.

Then there was a horrendous screech of metal on metal. His chest slammed into the steering wheel with bruising force, knocking the breath from his lungs. The momentum propelled the car to skid sideways and collide with the van again, this time from the rear. The collision sent his body smashing against the driver's door. Natalya's scream reverberated and then was abruptly cut off. His head cracked hard against the window. The last thing he remembered was the suffocating sensation of the deployed airbags.

Lucas rose and backed away from those bloody gloved hands doing God knows what to whoever was on that table. He bumped into another tray filled with instruments of torture and froze at the resultant clang. He covered his privates and met the startled gaze of the doc. Except, she looked right through him, her pretty green eyes narrowed with suspicion.

"That's not funny, Hank. I told you I don't like your games."

The man, Hank, threw his hands up in the classic 'hold on there' pose. "Hey, it wasn't me this time, I swear." He moved closer to the tools, as though to defend himself with a scalpel or something, the idiot.

The woman's eyes pierced the shadows, only marginally relaxing when she found the room empty.

Well, except for the stiffs and him of course. Lucas had a very bad feeling. The only reason for those two not to be able to see him was if he were invisible. And since he was reasonably sure he hadn't received a bite from a radioactive spider, he must be a... ghost.

No sooner did the thought flutter wraithlike through his mind than Lucas' feet lifted from the tiled floor, pulled up by a brilliant white light encircling his body. He groaned, the heat a benediction on his aching bones. So it was true, there was another realm after death. He'd always believed when he died, that was it. He'd become just another shit-stain on the fabric of mankind. It's how he'd lived his life, no harm, no foul. But, this. This felt... divine.

If there really was a heaven, he didn't deserve a spot. Not after everything he'd done.

It seemed like only seconds later the beam transported him to a textured surface sort of like the topping on his favorite dessert of lemon meringue pie. There were hills and hollows all in creamy shades of tan and white as far as the eye could see. It made him queasy.

He looked around but didn't see another soul, living or otherwise. Nice to know he hadn't lost his rather dubious sense of humor when he died.

Christ.

He was dead.

The stark truth hit him and drove him to his knees. Little tufts of cloud bounced crazily, temporarily obscuring his vision. Not that he was missing much; he was the only freaking person up here.

Was this his fate then? To spend an endless eternity wandering around the perimeter between this world and the next, not allowed to enter either dimension? It was no more than he deserved, but he'd give anything to know what happened to Scott, Natalya, and that family. He didn't care what lay in store for him as long as they were okay.

Please.

A sensation crept over his skin like a warm breeze. Someone was watching. His head flipped around like *Beetlejuice*, searching the ever-changing monochromatic landscape around him, but there was nothing.

And then, suddenly—there was.

A figure appeared out of the mist. Completely covered in a glowing white robe from head to toe, the ethereal body floated across the distance and came to a halt about a metre away. The... thing stood with its head bowed and arms crossed in front of him. He could have easily passed for an albino monk.

Holy shit.

If Lucas wasn't dead already, this place would have done the trick. He'd never been a fan of fun houses. The creepy mirrors, moving floors, and freaky characters appearing out of nowhere pretty much negated the whole *fun* aspect.

He rose on unsteady legs and waited, heart in his throat, ready to turn tail and run if that robe uncovered a creature from his nightmares.

"Who are you? Why am I here?" he demanded.

The guy rocking the bed sheet fashion accessories wasn't talking. Why was this happening? Okay, he got it. He'd fucked up, but it was a little late to do anything about it. If he was dead, fine. Drop him in a hole somewhere and leave him the hell alone.

This is bullshit.

"We agree."

The words, spoken in a soft baritone, seemed to enter his head without ever being uttered. Lucas raised his hands for protection against he knew not what. His heart threatened to bounce from his chest. He closed his eyes and prayed to a God who'd never listened that he was just in shock and this was all a bad dream. It had to be. But when he chanced opening them a few moments later, nothing had changed. It seemed this was to be his new reality.

"Come," the voice said. Without waiting on his compliance—though really, where was he going to go—the figure turned and drifted over a nearby peak.

Lucas hesitated, torn between throwing himself over the nearest cloud-bank, and trailing behind to see just what the future held in store for him.

Curiosity won. He followed.